Implications

Barbara Winkes

For D.

Chapter One

Ellie couldn't remember her workplace ever being this quiet. Experience had taught her that she should enjoy the relative peace, since it was likely the calm before another storm.

Calm was an accurate depiction of her state of mind these days. She felt happy and serene with recent decisions. While waiting for her report to print, she cast a look at the clock on the wall. Ten more minutes, then she and Jordan could go home.

Ellie shifted a few papers around on her desk, the clicking of keys in the background almost hypnotic. Jordan had been in with the lieutenant for a few minutes and was now finishing her own paperwork. Come to think of it, more desks than usual were occupied, except for Derek Henderson's. He had taken some time off to go on a honeymoon with Ellie's best friend Kate.

"Hey, there's no coffee around here? When is Henderson coming back?" Detective Maria Doss asked. She was coming in for the night shift.

"In a couple of weeks. They left *today*," Jordan answered, sharing an amused look with Ellie. "I don't know that you're going to need much. It's been slow."

"I still need coffee," Maria grumbled. "They're really going to spend their honeymoon camping in Canada?"

"It appears so. What's wrong with Canada?"

"There's nothing wrong with Canada. There's everything wrong with camping."

Jordan shrugged, obviously not in a mood to argue the point.

"Ellie, you're ready to go? I don't think much of importance will happen in the next five minutes."

Leaving his office, Lieutenant Carroll overheard Jordan's remark.

"I sure hope so, Carpenter. Enjoy your evening. Doss—pretend you don't have my number."

He looked ready to go to a fancy dinner or function, whistling as he left the building.

"Will do, boss," Maria said when he was out of earshot, sitting down at her desk to start her computer. "So, who's on duty tonight? I saw Casey earlier. That's good."

"I saw Atwood as well," Jordan told her. Maria made a face.

"Really, you just had to do that. Wish me luck, at least. Maybe I don't have to talk to him."

"Fingers crossed. Let's go, Ellie, I'm starving."

It was a rather innocent remark, but it made Ellie smile. Their plans weren't that advanced yet, but everything was coming together. After various tests and getting the green light from Jordan's doctor, they had to figure out one more detail.

They almost made it to the double doors when the woman walked inside. Ellie recognized her—a reporter who had once written a story about her. She and Jordan were off the clock now, so they'd let Maria handle whatever it was Jill Allen was here for. They had items on their private agenda to deal with. To Ellie's dismay, the reporter headed straight for her.

"Detective Harding, I'm so glad you're still here."

"Not for much longer, Ms. Allen. You can always talk to Detective Doss over there."

She could tell that Jordan was going into hovering mode—she probably had the same thought.

"If this is about Natalie Morgan, I have no comment." Ellie had decided that she'd treat the woman, who was now in prison, like any other criminal they'd apprehended. Case closed.

Allen looked surprised.

"No, that's not why I'm here. I'm sorry, that must have been painful...but we're not going to run a story on that. I wanted to talk to you about George Wilder."

The name rang a bell for Ellie though she couldn't put her finger on it.

"The old case about the dorm room murder?" Allen prompted.

"Wasn't there a story about that on TV, a couple of weeks ago?" Ellie remembered catching a segment of it.

"That's right. Mr. Wilder's sister approached me last week. Could we sit down and talk somewhere? Here, perhaps? It seems pretty quiet."

Truth be told, Ellie was curious—and grateful that the reporter didn't want to discuss how Natalie had fooled not only her, but most people Ellie cared about.

"We were just about to go to dinner, why don't you join us?"

"You're sure you want to be seen in public with me?" Allen joked.

"It's all good as long as there's food in the near future," Jordan said. "Let's go."

❦

Jill Allen barely waited until the waitress had filled their glasses with water and taken their orders.

"Doreen Byrd, that's the sister, gave me carte blanche to talk to you. George Wilder recently died in prison—of natural causes—and she's not in great health either which means we don't have a lot of time."

3

"We?" Ellie could tell that Jordan was skeptical.

"I need your help on this, obviously. She's convinced that he was innocent. He swore to her on his deathbed that he didn't kill the woman."

"What was their relationship?" Ellie asked, Jordan, almost at the same time, "Why does she think he told the truth?"

"Good questions, both of you." Allen admitted. "First of all, he was the victim's boyfriend at the time. Doreen insists that he loved her and would have never hurt her. George always claimed that he was innocent, but there was too much evidence pointing at him, and a lack of alternative suspects."

"When did this happen?" Ellie asked.

"In 1959."

"Okay." Jordan shook her head. "This is all very interesting, but what makes you think that our boss and the D.A. will want to re-open a case that was investigated and tried sixty years ago? Because of a deathbed proclamation of innocence? Maybe he wanted to protect his sister, or his reputation."

"That's a sad story, though. If he was innocent and in prison for all those years..."

"We don't know that. Besides, there is no time for this."

"You didn't look awfully busy when I came in...My apologies. That was uncalled for. Please, hear me out. You're good. I know you are. Detective Harding—"

"Call me Ellie, please."

"Okay, Ellie."

Jordan sighed.

"You could be clearing an innocent man's name. That would not only help your career, but show the community that you care..."

"Okay, now you're laying it on a bit thick. What's in it for you?"

"Nothing but truth and justice," Allen claimed. "We're on the same team here, aren't we? I keep thinking, what if someone I loved went to prison for a crime they didn't commit, their lives ended?"

"Well, we know about one life that was ended," Jordan said, her tone sharp. She caught herself.

"I'm sorry. I understand that this woman is looking for a way for all of this to make sense somehow, but I'm not sure that there's much we can do."

"I can look into it," Ellie offered. "Look, I've been shuffling papers around all day. Please, don't print that," she said to Allen, making her laugh.

"I would never! It's not the story I'm after. Besides, you all put some major league criminals away in the past few months. If you have a slow day, that means it's safe around here. I'd be so grateful if you could look at the case, see if anything strikes you as odd. I think that's all Doreen wants, that someone is taking this seriously."

Jordan kept an impassive expression. Ellie was well aware of the reporter's flattery. She might have to make it clearer that her means to work this case would be limited.

"I'll talk to my supervisor, and I'll get back to you with whatever I find. Don't promise anything to Mrs. Byrd yet. She might be disappointed."

"Thank you so much, Ellie. And it's Jill. I need to go now. Thank you for hearing me out."

"No problem, Jill."

"No problem, Jill?" Jordan echoed after she was gone.

"I didn't promise too much. Admit it, doing paperwork all day is what makes you grumpy. The lieutenant left work early, Kate and Derek are enjoying their vacation...For once, it's calm around here, so if there was ever a time to solve an old mystery, it's now."

"That sounds a bit too cozy. I saw that report too—if I remember correctly, the woman had her skull split open with an axe."

If the waitress had heard Jordan's words, her expression didn't show it as she put the plates on the table.

Ellie waited until she was gone.

"And thank you for always keeping it real. What if he didn't do it?"

⁂

Perhaps she'd overreacted a bit, Jordan reflected as she sat up against the headboard that night, Ellie sleeping next to her. She had watched Ellie closely in the past few days, after Natalie's arrest, watching for signs of, she wasn't sure what. It might be her own guilt, because she hadn't done more to prevent this disaster from happening. She hadn't voiced her suspicions earlier.

But Ellie seemed to be doing fine. She was processing, acknowledging her emotions, and she had her mind set on taking a closer look at the Wilder case.

Jordan hoped this wouldn't turn out to be a disappointment. The lieutenant wasn't likely to be on board with re-opening the investigation, and even if he was, Wilder might have been guilty. On the bright side, Allen might be right when she said this could turn out to be good for Ellie. Not all of the media had been as decent as Allen's employer. Jordan had caught a story or two online about the cops that got played by a clever criminal, but of course that was before they caught Natalie.

They had other, more pleasant things to think about anyway. The idea that she might be pregnant in a matter of weeks filled her with excitement and only a surprisingly small amount of panic. Movement beside her alerted Jordan that Ellie was awake and studying her.

"She's gone," Ellie said softly, as if reading her thoughts. Not that it was difficult—Natalie, and how to handle the aftermath of her deception, had been on her mind a lot. "I had a little meltdown over it. I felt I was entitled after the story she sold to us, but I'm okay now. Are you?"

"Yes. Of course."

Ellie sat up to face her.

"I swear, it's all good," she continued. "We caught her—well, technically April and her team did most of the work regarding Natalie, but Allen is right. We put away some heavyweights, and the city is safer for it. We are entitled to breathe. And the timing is pretty good."

"It is," Ellie confirmed, leaning into her. "If everything goes as planned...and there's no reason why it shouldn't," she added quickly. "I guess this announcement will make everyone forget about our glitch in judgment."

"Which is not the reason why we want to do this, but you have a point."

Thinking of some of the conversations she, they'd have in the future was a little less exciting to Jordan, but she felt confident she'd be able to handle them. Maybe, finally, Ellie's relentlessly hopeful outlook on life was rubbing off on her.

Chapter Two

It was with some regret that Ellie extracted herself from Jordan's embrace only a few hours later. She wanted to get to the station early. With a little luck, she could find something to present to the lieutenant that convinced him it was worth talking to the A.D.A.

Despite the interrupted sleep, she felt like she had a lot more energy than in recent days. After having to deal with Natalie, assessing and coping with the damage she'd done, Ellie welcomed the opportunity to focus on more important matters.

The baby plan, first and foremost.

Maybe, she'd have the opportunity to clear an innocent man's name.

The officer working in Records regarded her with wide eyes when she made her request.

"Wow. That was a long time ago. What you need might not even be in this building."

"Could you take a look?"

"Yes, of course. Give me a minute."

The woman typed something on her keyboard. She looked up at Ellie, giving her an apologetic smile. "You might want to sit down for a moment. First, we'll have to check if the file was already digitalized."

Ellie had to admit that she hadn't even considered these possible obstacles, but it made the case all the more intriguing.

"That's okay." She hadn't snuck out of bed at 5:30 for nothing. Ellie hid a yawn behind her hand.

"Okay, there's a file here. I can get it for you, but for the rest, you'll have to go to the Archives. They open at eight."

"Thank you, that's very helpful."

The officer disappeared behind a door, and Ellie was left alone. Ten minutes later, she had to sit up straighter in her chair to make sure she wouldn't fall asleep. Another five minutes later, the officer reappeared.

"I'm sorry about that," she said. "Can I get you anything else?"

"No, thanks. This is great. I'll go to the Archives later."

Ellie found Maria Doss at her desk. Her night seemed to have been fairly uneventful.

"Good morning. I take it you didn't have to notify the lieutenant about anything."

"Why are you here already? What's wrong with you?"

Ellie laughed. "I was just about to get myself a coffee. I take it you'd like one?"

"I shouldn't, as I'm going to a brunch later, but yes, please."

A few minutes later, Ellie was back, enjoying her coffee as she went over the specifics of the Wilder case.

These forms had been filled out on a typewriter. She noticed the names of the investigators, who would be long retired by now—or dead. She hoped she'd be able to find the retired ones and talk to them.

George Wilder was a twenty-year-old college student, accused of and convicted for killing his girlfriend Stella Brown after a party. He claimed he was innocent, but the evidence was damning: The murder weapon wrapped in a bloody shirt, hidden in the closet of his dorm room. There was the mention of a witness who had seen him go into Stella's room the night of the murder. Where was the motive? Some of their classmates suggested that jealousy might have been a reason, but if Stella had been seeing someone else, no one knew about it. It remained unclear whether this theory was valid.

Ellie assumed that she might find more information at the courthouse. Something about Wilder had made the jurors think that he had committed the atrocious crime. He had admitted that both he and Stella had been drinking, but that he'd said goodbye to her at the door to her dorm room and left. He appeared devastated over her death, and never confessed.

Ellie tried to imagine the scene, a young couple enjoying a night out together, going home to their respective dorms, then...what? Someone had stolen into Stella's room with an axe? That was a big risk. She might wake up, try to defend herself, scream...unless there had been more in her blood than alcohol.

She needed more of a background on both the victim and convicted suspect. She started to jot down notes—*Archives, Investigators, Family, Prison, Newspapers*—when a soft kiss to her neck alerted her to the fact that Jordan had finally made it to work. The gesture was tender and quick, but of course Maria had noticed.

"You two are so adorable, it's annoying," she said. "I'm out of here. Thanks for the coffee, Ellie, and good luck."

"So did you find anything?" Jordan was in a much better mood than she had been when Allen approached them about the case. Of course, she had slept longer and taken the time for breakfast. Ellie also prided herself in having to do something with Jordan's much improved spirits, including their conversation about the future and subsequent activities the previous night.

"It's too early to say, but for one, the motive is still unclear to me from what I've seen. I have a list of places to go."

"It will be tough to find most of the people involved at the time."

"Yeah, but we already have Doreen Byrd. She might be able to tell me where to find some of those people. And I want to talk to the prison employees. I'll take it up with the lieutenant when he comes in, and he'll hopefully agree that we talk to Valerie."

Jordan looked doubtful. Ellie thought that unfortunately, she had a reason—A.D.A. Esposito wouldn't follow along on a vague hunch, but Ellie needed her on her side.

"I can't help it," she said. "I keep thinking about what Jill said—what if it was someone we cared about? We can't just forget about it because it happened sixty years ago. There might be a murderer out there who's been enjoying his freedom while this man spent his life in prison."

"It's a shame if that's what happened. The system isn't perfect."

"Such dark thoughts on a beautiful morning," Valerie Esposito joked.

Ellie jumped to her feet.

"You're here! Could I talk to you for a second?"

"Actually, I was here to speak to your boss for a second, and then I have a working brunch later. If you could come to my office this afternoon?"

"Perhaps I could join you in the lieutenant's office? I swear this won't take long."

Lieutenant Carroll was already in the room, observing the scene with amusement.

"You see, Counselor, it's almost impossible to say no to Detective Harding. Five minutes."

"That's all I need for now. Thank you so much."

She sent a triumphant smile to Jordan before joining Carroll and Esposito.

Ellie usually got what she wanted. If there was anything new to find about this case, she'd find it.

❦

"I know it's been slow, but slow enough to look into a sixty-year-old case?" Carroll had doubts. Ellie had expected them.

"I'd like to talk to the family, and a few other people. Get a more complete picture. This man didn't seem to have any motive, yet he was convicted rather quickly."

"They must have had something on him."

"Evidence, and there was an eyewitness who put him at the scene," Ellie admitted. "However, the testing wasn't up to today's standards, much of what is routine right now wasn't even available. The murderer could still be out there."

"If they are, they might be Wilder's age or older," Valerie reminded her. "Still, you're right that we don't give criminals a pass just because they're older. I watched that segment a couple of weeks ago, and I have to admit, this case is puzzling. I would hate to see that someone dropped the ball, but if that was the case...someone should take responsibility."

Carroll sighed.

"I knew I was going to regret this. The sister, why did she come forward now?"

"Wilder swore to her on his deathbed that he didn't kill Stella Brown. He never confessed to the murder in the first place. Mrs. Byrd contacted a reporter, and she came to talk to me."

"If he really died an innocent man in prison, that's a grim story," Valerie said. "Of course, his family wants to believe him, but...I think if you have the time right now, we should look into it. Give her something. From a more cynical viewpoint, she won't sue. Not that she'd be likely to win at this point, but the optics wouldn't be good either."

"Okay, Harding. You have until the end of the week to produce some results, anything that looks like this is worth pursuing. If you can't come up with anything, I'll expect you back in the present by Friday."

"Thank you, sir."

Challenge accepted.

Ellie was well aware that Carroll hadn't given her a lot of time. If there was any emergency, he'd pull her back from the case, and even so, a few days were not a lot. She might be able to get a good idea of the possibilities.

She called Jill Allen to tell her the good news and asked if she could arrange a meeting with Doreen Byrd later that evening.

"She'll be happy to meet you, thank you so much! I didn't expect you to get back to me so soon."

"Well, I said I'd look into it. I know I wanted to hold off telling her, but there are some questions I need to ask."

"Sure. I'll text you the address. You'll be ready by seven?"

"I'll try to. See you later."

Ellie glanced at the list she had written earlier and decided to visit the Archives first. The people she'd meet would likely tell her all kinds of stories about Wilder, good and bad, but she needed to take a look at the evidence. She hoped she'd be able to drop by the prison in the afternoon and make a game plan with Allen. If there was still a plan after this day.

Jordan was on the phone, so she waved, left and got into her car. It occurred to her how much more relaxed the work atmosphere was since Waters, her first partner in Homicide, was gone. Previously partnered with Maria, he had always displayed bigoted attitudes, but not to the point that anyone could have him fired. That changed when he sexually assaulted a young officer who reported him.

He'd been mostly grumpy and condescending around Ellie. Now, everyone could take a deep breath. She had support from her colleagues when she needed it but was able to do her job.

At the Archives, a clerk took her down several stories and to a giant room with rows and rows of boxes on shelves high enough to use a ladder for the top ones.

"You should find everything you need in this area," he indicated one of the shelves at the end of the room. "Let me know if you need anything—I'll be at my desk."

It had already been hot when she left the department, but in these cool surroundings, Ellie wished she had brought a jacket with her. Nevertheless, she found the boxes related to the Wilder case, took out the first and opened it.

The murder weapon and the bloody shirt it had been wrapped in.

These were relicts of an action that had hardly come out of the blue, but from a person harboring extreme anger. If it was George Wilder who had hated Stella Brown this much, wouldn't there have been any hint in his behavior, his treatment of her? The file hadn't given her much, but perhaps Doreen Byrd could fill in some of the blanks.

Ellie spent a quiet pensive morning at the Archives. When she left the building and stepped back into the sunlight, she wasn't any wiser as to the motive for the brutal murder.

Re

The prison guard who had agreed to talk to her was about to take his lunch break. He offered Ellie that she could join him in the cafeteria. Given that her breakfast had consisted of coffee and a granola bar, she accepted.

"I take it you had known Mr. Wilder for quite a few years."

"Oh yes. I've been working here for almost fifteen."

"Tell me your impression, please."

Ellie nearly suppressed a sigh after the first bite of her ham sandwich. It was much better than she'd expected.

"If you want to know whether he was guilty or not, I can't tell you that. I'm sure you've seen a lot of criminals that are socially capable. But...I have to say he was what we call a model prisoner."

"Could you give me any more details?"

"Well, he was a young man when he was convicted. The time I knew him, he was always polite, never at the center of any trouble, tried to help others when he could."

"Did he ever mention to you the reason why he was convicted?"

"No, he didn't talk about that, ever. I guess he made his peace—due to the severity of the crime, he was convicted without parole."

"Who came to visit him?"

"Not many people," the guard said. "His sister, mostly, and his parents when they were still alive. I didn't meet them, but that's what I've been told. And there's an older lady who was a friend of his back then. I guess she believed him too."

"I need those names."

"You're very determined. I'll get them for you. A coffee first, before we go back?"

It took Ellie a moment to realize that his smile wasn't entirely out of professional courtesy.

"I'm sorry, I don't have much time. If you could get me those names now, you'll have time to come back for a coffee," she suggested.

"Sure. Please, feel free to come by if you need anything else."

Fifteen minutes later, Ellie was driving back to the station, the list of names on the passenger's seat next to her. She wasn't planning on coming back so soon.

Chapter Three

P eace and quiet didn't last that long. The shooting in a convenience store had left two men dead, the owner and a customer, with the shooter still on the run. Both victims had multiple gunshot wounds. One man lay sprawled behind the counter, the other one had fallen right next to the door.

Jordan assumed he'd tried to run.

As she carefully stepped over broken glass, she couldn't help but wonder how being pregnant would affect her day-to-day tasks on the job, the changes she'd have to make. It was obviously too early to mention anything to Lieutenant Carroll, but at some point, she wouldn't have a choice. Officer Casey Lyons was the only one of their close friends that had children while on the force, but since she was working the night shift at the moment, Jordan hadn't seen her this week. She hoped to find time to talk to her soon, get an idea of what to expect.

"Fortunately, there was no one else in the store at the time of the shooting." Officer Libby Marshall winced. "Not that this isn't bad enough."

"It sure is bad," Jordan agreed. She kneeled next to one of the bodies, donning gloves before she picked up the handgun that lay only inches from the store owner's hand and carefully placed it in an evidence bag. "He was trying to defend himself."

"Looks like it. I have a couple of witnesses that heard the shots," Libby said. "Four or five at least. Then they saw the man storming out. White, late twenties to early thirties, wore a green sweater and jeans."

"Any hint it could be gang-related?"

"It could be it's too damn easy for people to get their hands on guns," Libby muttered.

Dr. Adams, the medical examiner, shrugged. "Not to tell you how to do your jobs, but I'll go out on a limb to say that the murder weapon was probably not legally obtained."

Jordan wasn't going to walk into that conversation, especially at this early stage.

"Well, let's get this one to the lab and see what it can tell us. And we need to get that description out. Have those witnesses come to the station—and I need a few more uniforms to comb the neighborhood. Maybe we're lucky and the guy didn't get far.

She had a fleeting thought for her partner Derek Henderson who was enjoying his camping trip with his wife...Jordan wished them well, but she agreed with Maria on the subject. The idea of camping wasn't at all intriguing to her, not as much as catching the bad guys.

<hr>

Ellie had been able to move her meeting with Jill, and Doreen Byrd, up an hour after Jordan suggested they'd see Jack and Pauline for dinner. At the same time, they'd be able to take a look at the progress made in the rebuilt *Code 7*. The bar had been a popular hangout for cops until it was destroyed by a criminal with delusions of grandeur. Jordan's dad got together with a couple of friends and bought the property to build the bar from the ground up. According to the latest news, they were almost ready to open.

Jack and Pauline didn't know yet that soon they'd have something else to celebrate.

When Doreen Byrd opened the door, Ellie could tell that the woman wasn't in best health. Grief had probably worsened her condition.

"Welcome, Detective Harding. You have no idea how grateful I am you're doing this."

Ellie endured the surprisingly firm, bordering-on-desperate handshake.

"For now, I have gathered some information and asked some questions. In fact, I have many questions for you."

They sat down in the living room where Jill Allen was already waiting. Mrs. Byrd produced a box of letters and held it out to Ellie.

"I trust you with these. George wrote them from prison." Tears were forming in the corners of her eyes. "He didn't do this. He wasn't capable."

"How much do you remember about the murder?" Ellie asked.

"I was in college when it happened, but of course I came home when George was arrested. I had met Stella on a few occasions. They were in love, talking about getting married, having a family. Someone took that away from both of them."

"I'm sorry, but I have to ask this—why now?"

"We have tried so many things over the years, paid for lawyers, and private investigators, even DNA testing when it was available. Someone framed my brother, but we couldn't find proof. You are my last chance."

Ellie caught Jill's gaze on her. *No pressure.*

"Jill told me that George swore to you he didn't kill Stella."

"That's right. In the recent years, he didn't want to talk about it at all, so I was surprised when he brought it up again days before his death." She wiped her eyes. "He said now that he's going to join Stella, it's important that the world knows."

"All right. I'm going to talk to some of the investigators on the original case, and I also saw the prison guard earlier. He gave me a list of visitors that your brother had. Could you take a look for me?"

"Yes, of course, but I'd be surprised if there were names besides mine. People made up their minds very quickly."

That had been Ellie's impression as well. She waited while Mrs. Byrd looked at the short list. "This was the private investigator. He went by himself a couple of times and spoke to me after. Enid, of course. There's George's lawyer. He took over the practice from his dad a while ago."

"The guard told me Enid Montgomery was an old friend?"

"Yes. She started visiting him a few years after he was convicted. I guess she wasn't sure in the beginning. This was a shock for everyone. Stella and Enid were friends too. They had been to our parents' house a lot."

Ellie remembered the vague theory that jealousy might have caused a rift in the couple, that eventually led to the murder. Had George cheated on Stella? Or had Stella? If there had been more than friendship between the women, they might be looking at a hate crime. But in that case, why was Enid visiting George? There were multiple possible interpretations, and sadly for Doreen Byrd, none of them looked too good for the man originally convicted.

"George and Enid were friends—nothing else?"

"If there was anything else, I don't know, but I can't imagine it. She was a bookworm, always studying. She didn't seem to have any interest in dating."

Doreen was only two years older than her brother. Ellie thought that perhaps, Enid didn't have an interest in dating men...or she had and hidden it well. She and George could have planned the murder together, though that brought her back to the lack of a motive.

"I'll talk to her, in any case."

"Yes, you do that. Perhaps she can give you some other names, friends from that time."

"Do you happen to have her address?"

"Oh, sure. She still lives in her parents' house."

Ellie wrote down the address and got to her feet. Tomorrow, she'd see Enid Montgomery, and hopefully find out more about the original investigators, Patterson and Riley.

Now, for some family time.

⁂

Jordan had met her parents at the site of the new *Code 7*, where Ellie would join them later. She walked around the spacious place, admiring the progress. Jack and his friends had made some updates but managed to modernize the space without taking away its comfort. She had been coming here for years before it all went down in ashes. The original *Code 7* was associated with specific important memories.

"How is Ellie doing?" Pauline asked, and Jordan, who was still going through memories of the first times she'd met Ellie here, had a hard time keeping the smile off her face.

"She's good. You know Ellie. She doesn't dwell." In fact, Jordan was fairly proud of herself for trying, and mostly succeeding, to do the same.

She'd had moments of wondering whether it was selfish wanting to have the baby when Ellie was younger and wanted this child just as much. One of them would have to slow down their career either way. But Ellie had told her that she was on board with this decision one hundred percent, and she needed to trust her.

"No, she doesn't. What about you?"

"Dwelling? Me? No way." Jordan laughed. "We all feel a lot better since Natalie was arrested. It's over. We have other things to think about."

Pauline didn't ask, but maybe she had a sixth sense about these things. Jordan wouldn't put it past her.

"This is all looking great," she said, running her hand along the edge of the shiny new pool table. "When will it be open?"

"A few more weeks," Jack said, beaming at the prospect. "The local paper has promised to send someone. I also talked to Carl—he wishes us luck, though he's still devastated about everything that happened."

"I can imagine."

The son of Carl Roth, the *Code 7*'s former owner, had hated the place so much he'd taken drastic measures. Jordan suppressed a shiver. As many good memories as she had associated with the bar, there were a lot of bad ones where Danny Roth was concerned.

"But yeah, everything is going well on this end. So, you like it?"

"I love it!"

Ellie had come in, looking in awe.

"I can't wait until we can come here on a regular basis! It's even better than before."

"Well, maybe not every little detail," Jordan mumbled, secretly pleased that it got Ellie flustered. One particular experience, they wouldn't repeat. They had a home together, not to mention Jordan's parents now owned the place.

"All right," Pauline said. "Who wants to go for dinner?"

Ellie spent another early morning at her desk, going over George Wilder's file, reading the original reports again. Patterson and Riley were the detectives on the case. She found out that Detective Patterson was since deceased. There was an obituary from three years ago. She had tracked down Riley in a retirement community too far away for a day trip. She'd call him to figure out if he had anything for her that she needed to address in person.

As she flipped through the file once more, she realized there was a third name. She closed her eyes for a moment, hoping that she had imagined it, or, at best, that this might be a strange coincidence. A Detective Waters had signed off on one of the reports.

She did the math quickly. Her former partner hadn't been born yet, but it was entirely possible that this Waters was his father. That would be uncomfortable, to say the least. She wasn't even sure if she'd be able to talk to him in case she still needed to testify against him.

"Crap," she muttered, causing the officer who just walked by to give her a quizzical look. Ellie knew she didn't have a lot of time, but she decided to stall for a bit anyway. Talk to Riley first, then try to set up something with Enid Montgomery. Perhaps it wouldn't be necessary to involve Cliff Waters—either because she'd find something important without him, or because Lt. Carroll would shut down her investigation first.

Would Doreen Byrd be satisfied because Ellie had tried?

She called the retirement home, and a friendly staff member got her Riley on the line. To Ellie's relief, he remembered the Wilder case.

"Yes, of course, the college kid sneaking into his girlfriend's dorm room with an axe. One of the worst scenes, blood and brains everywhere." He paused. Ellie wasn't sure for what reason. "I saw that he died. Is that why you're calling?" Did he sound uncomfortable?

"I've been asked to look into the case," Ellie said. "Back then, did you have any doubts that he did it?"

"I assume you read the file, at least I hope you wouldn't call me without reading it first. We found the murder weapon in his room, and we had a witness that saw him go into her room. They had a big fight earlier."

"Doreen Byrd thinks he was framed."

"And this is the first time ever you heard that line from the murder suspect's family? How long have you been a Homicide detective?"

Ellie chose to take it as a rhetorical question.

"What about that witness?"

"Anonymous call, a woman. She was afraid. But you know that too."

"Yeah...with all the people you interviewed, you never identified her?"

"Well, that would be in the file, too. We might not have all the means you have today, but we knew detective work." He was a bit impatient now...and, Ellie sensed, still uncomfortable.

"The other investigators on the case were Detectives Patterson and—"

"I hope you'll let him rest in peace. We did everything by the book."

"I don't doubt that. Can you tell me about Detective Waters?"

"He came in when Patterson was shot, an unrelated case."

"That must have been tough...changing partners under such circumstances?"

"We weren't running a self-help group," he scoffed. "We were friends. He was old-fashioned, but a good cop."

The old-fashioned part, unfortunately, was making her theory more likely.

"Is there anything you'd like to add to what is in the file—about Wilder, about your investigation? If anything, this could give Mrs. Byrd some closure."

"You're wasting your time, in my opinion. Besides, we were more concerned with giving the Browns closure."

"I understand. Thank you for talking to me."

Ellie ended the call, doubting even more she'd have something good to present to the lieutenant by the end of the week. The Browns, of course, were on her list, and so was the lawyer who had taken over the practice from his father.

So far, everyone but Doreen seemed to be convinced that George Wilder had committed the gruesome crime. She couldn't wait to hear from his long-time friend Enid.

Chapter Four

B y noon, there was still no sign of the man in the green
sweatshirt, though the witnesses had come in to give their
description. At least, Jordan had some more information on the
victims—the owner, Ken Gentry, and the customer, Preston
Lucas. Gentry had taken over the store ten years ago from the
previous owner and kept it consistently in the red. Lucas lived
in an apartment building three blocks down the road. Chances
were he was a regular customer. He had also worked at various
times in the store, handling deliveries, filling the shelves, a little
bit of everything.

The two victims knew each other—did they also know their
killer, or was this a random act of violence?

She attended the autopsy of Gentry, but unfortunately
didn't learn much she hadn't already guessed.

Dr. Adams asked about Derek's whereabouts, looking a tad
disappointed when Jordan told her that he was on his honeymoon.

"Too bad all the good ones are taken. Men and women."

Jordan decided that she had nothing to add to that conversation.

"Well, thank you anyway. I'll wait for your report."

"Yeah. I'm afraid I won't have that much to add. Maybe
better luck with ballistics."

"Let's hope so."

Jordan went back to her desk to start her own preliminary report. Carroll would want to hear something from her today. After a few minutes, her phone rang, and she picked up.

"This is Detective Carpenter."

"Detective Shriver, Major Crimes."

That gave her pause. Her last interaction with Major Crimes had been when their lieutenant interviewed her as a witness. The meeting had been cautiously friendly. This was too late to be a follow-up.

"How can I help you?"

"I thought maybe I could help you. I have a home invasion on my hands, in broad daylight. Guy shot the husband. Fortunately, he'll make it."

"That's...good."

"I agree. Perp got away with some credit cards and jewelry. They also said he was wearing a green sweatshirt with dark stains on it."

"Wow." Jordan was on her feet the next moment. "I have a facial composite here of someone I bet they'll recognize. We're lucky he didn't kill them too. When and where can I meet you?"

"Oh, I was hoping you'd say that. I'm still at the hospital. If you come over here now, you could show that facial composite to Mrs. McDonald."

"Give me fifteen minutes and call me again if there's a hit on any of those credit cards."

"Sure. See you."

It looked like she'd have something to tell the lieutenant after all. With a little luck, she could even present a suspect. The day was looking up.

She had a doctor's appointment coming up, too.

It was both strange but thrilling to think that she and Ellie would be looking at potential donors.

Baby steps.

⟨⟩

Before visiting George and Stella's friend Enid, Ellie called the number for Wilder's lawyer, only to learn that the father had died years ago, and his son who owned the practice, was out of the country for at least another two weeks. She made a note and went on her way.

Enid Montgomery, seventy-nine, lived by herself in the small cottage-style house that had belonged to her parents. It didn't look like much had been changed after her parents' deaths, or even before. The wallpaper and the décor looked like something out of the 1950s, and heavy curtains gave the place a slightly claustrophobic feel.

She had, however, prepared coffee, and set out a plate of delicious looking cookies when Ellie arrived.

"Thank you for meeting me. You didn't have to do that, though."

"Oh, please, don't insult me." Ms. Montgomery smiled. "Sit, dear, and have some of those cookies. I won't lie—I was looking forward to your visit. Doreen says hello every once in a while, but she is very busy."

"I'd like to talk to you about George Wilder."

Ellie sat and picked up the cup. The coffee was stronger than she had expected.

"Oh yes, George. What a tragedy."

"You went to see him in prison often."

"Not in the beginning. No one knew what to think, you know? My best friend was dead. I couldn't see clearly."

"I understand," Ellie said softly. She was happy that Kate had found love again, but on the worst day, Ellie and other fellow officers had lost a friend as well. However, there had been no doubt as to who had killed Jensen Baker. Was there really any doubt in Wilder's case, or had Doreen Byrd's grief clouded her judgment? "But at some point, you started seeing him. What changed?"

Enid Montgomery regarded her with curiosity.

"Can I ask why you're so interested in the story? Why now?"

"If you are talking to Doreen, you might know that she approached a reporter after George died. They are sure that he didn't commit the murder, and if that's true, law enforcement needs to be involved."

"I guess you're right about that. Do you believe in forgiveness?"

The question startled Ellie more than she'd admit. In the past few years she'd met plenty of people that were far beyond forgiveness. Others, in a somewhat grey zone. But Wilder had never shown remorse. In fact, he had insisted he was innocent.

"Do you? Is that why you visited him?"

Montgomery pondered the question for a few long seconds.

"To be honest? I don't know," she said. "Maybe, eventually, I did. He was always such a polite, soft-spoken man. Maybe I wanted to believe him. And then there were days when I wasn't sure, and I went to assure myself that they'd keep him in there for the rest of his life."

Enid Montgomery had been very young at the time of the crime. Ellie didn't blame her for having mixed feelings, yet she felt there had to have been something more to those frequent visits.

"What did you talk about?"

She answered with a dismissive gesture. "Anything and nothing. I'm afraid none of this will be of much help to you. He always asked me to describe the weather and the season in detail. He asked me about my day, and told me about his..." She laughed wryly. "Sometimes it was hard to tell whose was more boring."

"You have lived all your life in this house."

"Yes. I went to college about an hour away." Asking people uncomfortable questions was part of her job, though Ellie hesitated anyway. Ms. Montgomery didn't make it any easier on her, waiting as well.

"You never married?"

"Well, the right one never came along. Are you married, my dear?"

"Actually, yes. Could you tell me about Stella?" While Ellie couldn't have been prouder or happier, she didn't think her own private life belonged in this conversation.

"Stella was…" Ms. Montgomery's voice turned almost dreamy as she continued. "Exceptional. She was smart, and beautiful, always got what she wanted. Such a brilliant light put out, it's a shame." Her eyes were welling up. Still, Ellie couldn't stop there.

"How much do you remember about that night? You were all at a party together?"

Enid hesitated, as if she was gathering her thoughts. Her answer was surprisingly specific. Ellie assumed that she'd thought about that night a great deal over the past decades.

"Yes. I didn't really care, but George asked me to come. He thought I should take some time to enjoy myself, so I changed my mind." Ellie could only describe the woman's smile as mischievous. "I assume you can guess that there was alcohol, even though we weren't supposed to drink."

"I can imagine." It had to be strange when your best memories were so close to the worst—then again, Ellie knew a bit about that too.

"I left before them, though. I know that George claimed he said goodbye to Stella at the front door, though I know he often went with her and snuck out in the middle of the night. She told me."

"You lived at the same dorm?"

"Yes, but my room was on another level. I was much too far away to be able to hear or see anything."

"Okay. Ms. Montgomery, I'd like to ask you one more question. In your opinion, why would George, or anyone, hate Stella this much?"

The woman shook her head. "I'm sorry, but I have no answer for you. Why would anyone hate her? She was perfect. Wait. I want to show you something." She got up and went into another room. Ellie could hear her open a cabinet door. Enid returned a couple of minutes later. "Here. See for yourself."

Ellie noted Enid must have kept the yearbook close to be able to find it right away, a memento of a time long gone that obviously mattered a great deal to her. She had to agree. Most of the pictures, including Enid's and George's, were fairly unremarkable for young adults of their time. She could only describe Stella's as stunning. No wonder everyone had been drawn to her.

"I can tell you understand it now. Can I help you with anything else?"

In fact, Ellie had another question left, but she decided that would be for another day.

"I think this is all for now. Thank you very much for taking the time, Mrs. Montgomery."

"It was my pleasure, dear. Please come back if you need anything else."

At least, someone else was as bewildered as to George's motive.

Had somebody framed him? But why?

While her husband was in surgery, Detective Noah Shriver introduced Jordan to Mrs. McDonald. She'd been treated for shock but was physically unharmed. When Jordan showed her the facial composite created from the witness's description of the man in the green sweatshirt, she didn't hesitate.

"That's him! I'll never forget that face. He didn't wear a mask or anything...I thought he was going to kill both of us!"

"I'm sorry, Mrs. McDonald," Jordan said softly. "He was alone?"

"Yes. We were having lunch in the sunroom...He was there all of a sudden, waving the gun in our faces."

"He stole their car too," Shriver said. "We got a BOLO out, and roadblocks in place. He's not going to get far." The last part was almost a whisper, meant for Jordan only. She nodded. What they didn't need to spell out was that this man had already killed two and seriously injured another man. He had to know that they were getting closer. He might feel cornered.

"Had you ever seen him before?"

Jordan's question elicited a small, amused smile from Shriver, before he caught himself. Of course, he would have already asked that question. The perp's act was likely out of desperation, but there might be some small chance that his crimes were connected to a concerted effort.

"If I did, I don't remember. But I'm certain now."

"Okay. Thank you."

They heard footsteps behind them and turned around. The lieutenant of Major Crimes had arrived, waving Shriver over. Jordan went as well.

"What do we have?"

"Mrs. McDonald here identified a guy who's a suspect in a Homicide case. By the way, Detective Carpenter, meet Lieutenant Daniels."

"We've met," the lieutenant said as she and Jordan exchanged a polite smile. "You have a name?"

"Not yet. Homicide is still looking for witnesses."

She cast a quick look at Mrs. McDonald a few feet away, who was looking lost and forlorn.

"What's the status of the other victim?"

"In surgery, but he'll be okay."

"Good. Make sure no one else gets shot or killed by this guy. Good to see you again, Detective."

"You too."

"What was that all about?" Shriver asked when his supervisor was out of earshot.

"The shooting at the D.A.'s office. I'm sure you remember."

"Yes, of course. Homicide is always in the heat of the action." He corrected himself before Jordan could. "I'm sorry, that was uncalled for."

"Yes, it was, but quick save."

"Since we're joining forces on this one, let me buy you a coffee while we have a moment? I told the doctor to call me the moment Mr. McDonald wakes up...or, in case of something that hopefully doesn't happen."

"I could use some caffeine," Jordan agreed, realizing that there would come a moment when she wouldn't be able to indulge the way she had in all her adult life. But it would be worth it. "Let's quickly update dispatch now that those cases are related for sure."

36

"I was in Missing Persons for a few years," Jordan said, surprising herself. She hadn't talked about that part of her life, to anyone, in a long time. It had been Bethany who pushed for the change, and she hadn't been wrong. There were rarely false hopes in her day job, and it suited her. Yet, Ellie, who had a much sunnier disposition, wanted to be there.

"I can see why you wanted to be part of Carroll's gang. You guys have a reputation." Noah Shriver said it without scorn. He had a point.

"Our perps rarely get out quickly, if at all, unless they truly turn their lives around. There's a finality that matches the crime...I'm good with that."

"As long as you catch the right guy, I guess it's a good philosophy to live by," he acknowledged. "You think there's going to be any trouble with the case of the detective that was let go?"

"Why am I getting the impression there is an agenda behind all those casual questions?"

"Damn, am I that obvious? Apparently." He took a sip of his coffee, and before he could answer Jordan's question, both of their phones rang, a split-second apart.

Jordan's call came from Casey Lyons who was pursuing the McDonalds' vehicle with Officer Sam Potts. Shriver must have gotten the same information.

"All right, break's over," he said. "We should do this again sometime soon, continue that conversation."

"Sure. Another time."

❧

The driver brought the car to a screeching halt, walled in by buildings, a couple of squad cars and Jordan's car. Detective Shriver arrived seconds after her. They were taking cover behind the vehicles as everyone waited for the suspect to get out. Several commands by Casey had gone unanswered.

"Come on, get your ass out of there," Shriver mumbled. "I have places to be."

"Lighten up. He hasn't fired a shot—that's good news," Jordan reminded him.

"Yeah. For now."

Casey demanded once more for the suspect to exit the vehicle, and this time, he obeyed. He opened the door and got out, raising his hands above his head.

"Don't fucking shoot me!" he yelled. "I did nothing wrong!"

"And in what universe would that be?" Jordan shook her head.

"I guess we'll figure it out soon."

"The we being figurative, right? Because this guy is ours now."

"That appears to be another conversation we'll have to have later."

Chapter Five

"I hope you bring me good news, Harding," Carroll commented after he'd called Ellie into his office. He'd been on the phone when she'd first knocked.

"That depends…"

"Not sure I like the sound of that."

"I have more people to talk to, but the interviews I did today cast some doubt on Wilder's guilt," she explained as she sat in the visitor's chair. "I spoke to the prison guard and a woman who was a friend of his and the victim's. Even one of the original investigators had to admit that they didn't have much to go on."

She hadn't missed Carroll raising his eyebrows.

Ellie realized she'd have to give him more to support her theory. "Well, the axe wrapped in the bloody shirt—I'm aware I haven't been here for long, but that's almost too obvious, isn't it? It's like when we found Stanton with the bloody knife."

"Maybe, maybe not. Frankly, that's not a lot in favor of re-opening the case either. What about the other detectives, could you get a differing opinion?"

"Not yet…" Ellie suppressed the urge to fidget in her chair.

"What exactly does that mean?"

"One of them has passed, and the other one…is a Detective Waters. Cliff Waters' Dad. He lives in a retirement home. They said I have to get consent to talk to him."

"Right."

"I mean, the case is over, Cliff took a deal, and this has nothing to do with my testimony…"

"No, it doesn't, but I don't like the optics of it either."

A knock on the door interrupted their conversation, and a moment later, Jordan walked in, looking pleased with herself.

"Sir, I just wanted to let you know we arrested a suspect in the robbery on Baker. He wants a lawyer, so I can't talk to him right now, but we'll set something up for tomorrow."

"Good work, Carpenter."

While Ellie was happy to see her wife at any time, in this instance, the timing wasn't great.

"Thanks. He tried to get away in the car of the couple whose house he broke into, and the wife identified him earlier. It's solid."

"Sounds good to me. Please, stay for a moment." Carroll turned back to Ellie. "How important is it to get that second opinion? Do you think it makes sense to go down that route?"

Ellie pondered that question. If Waters was anything like his son, he might have been the one to quickly proclaim Wilder guilty. But there wasn't much else for her to insist on continuing her inquiries either way. She hoped to find something she could bring up at her next visit with Enid Montgomery. Ellie felt like the woman had more to contribute, and if she presented her with more details, she might be able to jog something in her memory.

The thought of going back to the house made her uncomfortable, even though the cookies had been tasty.

"I'd like to give it a shot, sir."

Lieutenant Carroll sighed.

"I trust your judgment on this, but if we need to go via your former colleague, I don't want you to go near him."

Jordan looked on with interest.

"Carpenter, when's that meeting with the lawyer? Bring Harding up to date, so she can follow up if necessary. See if you can get consent to talk to Waters' father about the Wilder case."

"Oh...okay."

"This is an exception," Carroll warned. "Get me some results."

"Of course," Ellie was quick to say.

"Good. Now get to work."

After they'd left the office, Jordan followed Ellie to her desk. She would have been happy to help with any of her cases...or at least that's what she had thought until Ellie managed to unearth a connection their former colleague had with a sixty-year-old case, however worth pursuing.

She had enough on her hands with the suspect, caught red handed stealing the McDonalds' car, after robbing them. The man had insisted on his innocence.

"He didn't want to go on without a lawyer, but he said he'd done nothing wrong. Wow. I guess we can all go home."

"Yeah. I'm sorry that happened. I didn't think the lieutenant would be so adamant about me staying away from Waters."

"What did you expect? You testified against him. I'm sorry," Jordan said with a sigh. "It occurred to me that I'll go nine months without caffeine. I'll better get it while I can. Come with me?"

"Sure."

Ellie got up to follow her into the break room where Jordan surprised her with a quick kiss.

"For my apology. And because I haven't seen you all day."

"Works for me."

"Okay. What do I need to know?" Jordan asked, filling quarters into the vending machine.

"I wish there was more, but here it is: Riley and Patterson were the original investigators. Patterson got shot during an unrelated assignment, and Waters senior stepped in. In my opinion, they closed the case very quickly, and Riley got a tad defensive when I talked to him on the phone this morning. I'd like to speak to Cliff's dad. As you've heard, we need to ask consent."

"So, Cliff Waters is the guardian? What does that mean?" Jordan tried not to sound too pessimistic, but she was fairly certain Carroll would shut down the investigation before the end of the week.

"I'm not sure. It means we have to ask him first, you, to be precise—and perhaps he remembers his dad talking about the case. I found a number of newspaper articles, and there was the TV segment, so who knows what we can shake loose."

"I'll see what I can do," Jordan promised.

"Thanks. Your turn."

"All right. You want anything?"

"Oh no. I had coffee and cookies at Mrs. Montgomery's."

"Lucky you. As I said earlier, we caught the guy driving the couple's car. Mrs. McDonald identified with from the facial composite we did with the witnesses of the robbery—it should be an open-and-shut case."

"But you're not sure?"

"There's a backlog in ballistics, but he did shoot Mr. McDonald. If he keeps arguing he did nothing wrong, he's either acting, or we need to bring in a psychiatrist. Give me a second, please?"

Jordan checked her phone and saw she'd received a message from Shriver. *Mr. McDonald woke up from surgery, backs up wife's story,* she read.

"Good," she said. "That's it for now—but I don't think I'll spend that much time with Waters anyway...if he lets me in at all."

"Try. You can be very charming, you know."

Jordan laughed. "Thanks...Not sure it will work on him, but we'll see."

⁓

"So, that appointment is coming up," Ellie stated once they were home. They had bought pizza on the way. Ellie had insisted on not having wine or beer, in solidarity. Not that anyone was pregnant—yet. With a little luck, and more science, Jordan would be. The idea still felt quite abstract to her, even though she'd been watching her diet since before the first tests. Her prospects were as good as they could be at her age, and for the umpteenth time, she asked herself if they'd made the right decision.

But she couldn't imagine not trying, and Ellie supported her in every possible way, so perhaps she already had all the answers she needed.

"Yes, it is."

"You know I'll go in with you, right?"

"Yeah...I imagined you would."

Ellie held her gaze, amused. "You're not nervous about it? I'll be there when you actually have the baby. And besides, I have seen you naked. Often."

As usual, her easygoing approach went a long way to disperse Jordan's doubts. She couldn't help laughing. "Context matters, okay? Yes, sure, maybe I am," she continued, more serious. "I know we made a decision. I want this, more than I ever imagined. And I'm afraid it might not work out."

"Why?"

"There are a ton of reasons, but one of them is…age."

"Women older than you have babies every day," Ellie reasoned. "I know that might sound like a weird thing to say, but it's true. And even if that was a problem, there are a few more options. We could adopt. We could still do that at some point in the future."

"God, I love you so much. I wouldn't be anywhere near figuring this out if it wasn't for you."

"I don't know that it's true but thank you."

There was one more thing that had been on Jordan's mind, on and off. She had avoided dealing with it so far. For one, it involved Kathryn, and if that wasn't enough, it was a scary thought even knowing Ellie was with her every step of the way.

"When Kathryn and I had that first serious talk…" She didn't have to go into more details. Ellie certainly remembered the occasion. "She told me that she had a miscarriage before she had me."

"That doesn't mean it will happen to you." Ellie's gaze was calm. She didn't seem surprised, by the revelation or the fact that Jordan had kept this detail from her.

"I swear I was going to tell you, and you're right. It's just that back then, I was so angry at her, and later, it seemed strange to bring up the subject. I think I should ask her if it's something that runs in the family."

"I understand you want to know."

"You think it's not a good idea?"

"I don't know what she's going to tell us, but if you want to go, let's say, tomorrow, I'll make time."

Just like that. *Us.* It came naturally, unlike in any other relationship Jordan had had in her adult life.

"Okay. Thank you."

"I don't want to be judgmental but remember that she was very young...and the circumstances probably weren't the best. Whatever it is, we'll deal with it."

It occurred to Jordan that this was the most optimistic she had ever been for the future. It was a new and exciting feeling, even with some potentially complicated conversations ahead.

⁓

However, Kathryn wasn't first on her list the next morning, but the suspect in two violent crimes, a man named Eric Driscoll. He had prepared his statement with his lawyer and was ready to talk. She nodded to James McKenzie, the attorney. Jordan had been fairly surprised to learn that he was representing Driscoll.

McKenzie liked the multi-layered cases that could go either way in a split-second. Only this wasn't one. Driscoll didn't have a criminal record, but he'd been seen running from the store where he'd shot two people and then identified by the McDonalds. There wasn't a plausible story that could save him.

"Okay, let's begin."

She knew that A.D.A. Esposito was on the other side with Ellie.

"We can keep this short, Detective," McKenzie said. "My client feared for his life. His mistake was that he was trying to flee from the scene both times, rather than call for help."

Jordan refrained from rolling her eyes, barely. Driscoll couldn't be so naïve to think he would get away with this? And McKenzie? What was his deal?

"I must admit I didn't expect this. You have to do better, Mr. Driscoll. Two people are dead."

"Gentry and Lucas wanted to set me up. They asked me to come to the store to talk. The moment I came in, Lucas pulled a gun on me."

"So, you knew both of them."

"Yes, of course. Lucas and I had worked odd jobs for both Gentry and McDonald. We knew too much, that's why they wanted us gone."

At this point, Jordan was quite sure that engaging in this fiction was a sad waste of taxpayer money. For sure, there was no reason why a well-off businessman and his wife *couldn't* be criminals, but Mr. McDonald was recovering from a gunshot wound, and Mrs. McDonald had been believably traumatized.

"Sorry, that's not how this works. Let me know when you're ready to tell the truth."

"Jordan...Detective Carpenter." James had jumped to his feet. "I promise you, you will want to hear this. I know it sounds outlandish, but there's something there. Mr. Driscoll."

"The store was in the red, but if you looked at some of the papers, you'd find a lot of inconsistencies. They were cleaning money for the McDonalds."

Jordan remembered a basic inquiry into Gentry's finances. She hadn't found any red flags yet.

"Those are some severe accusations. Do you have proof?"

"Like you said, two people are dead."

"What happened at the store?"

"Gentry and Lucas got into an argument. Gentry shot Lucas and aimed at me. I was only trying to defend myself!"

"Right, then you ran from the store and went on to rob the McDonalds next? You see how your story isn't making much sense?"

"They want to frame me! I took the car, yes, but I didn't rob them."

"So, Mr. McDonald shot himself?" Jordan asked, not bothering to hide the sarcasm.

"She did. They're in on it together. Afterwards, I'm sure she trashed the place to make it look like a robbery. You were already looking for me—so she knew you would believe her."

"Okay. We'll be looking into that."

"That's all?" Driscoll asked incredulously. He was about to get to his feet, but McKenzie laid a hand on his shoulder. "You did well. Let me handle this." To Jordan he said, "Mr. Driscoll has a point. We need to know you're taking this seriously. The McDonalds might be in the process of destroying evidence as we speak."

"Thank you for your statement, Mr. Driscoll."

Outside the room, Jordan had expected the surprised looks from Ellie and A.D.A. Esposito. What she didn't expect was to see Detective Shriver.

"You don't believe him?"

To be honest, Jordan didn't want to. "That's one elaborate story to come up with."

"Yes, because he wants to save his hide."

"I already told Detective Shriver that I'd prefer for you to rule out that elaborate story or confirm it," Esposito said. "Let me know what you find."

"You're not serious."

"Do I sound like I'm not serious, Detective? Since you've already worked on this, it should be quick to check."

Jordan excused herself when her phone rang. Ballistics had found inconsistencies regarding her first theory that made Driscoll the sole guilty party: There had been three shots fired from Gentry's gun, only one from Driscoll's. Had he used another weapon when robbing the McDonalds, or was his story actually true?

Chapter Six

Initially, Jordan had assumed that Gentry living above his means in a spacious condo had contributed to the failing of his store. The story was starting to change, she reflected, standing next to the safe they'd found hidden in the basement. It was open now, revealing stacks of bills, and folders filled with papers.

With gloved hands, Jordan had picked up one of the folders and leafed through it. Already, the first few pages turned out to be copies of checks, some signed by Gentry, some by—surprise—Mr. and Mrs. McDonald. The combinations of letters and numbers on another page could be codes or passwords.

"You look like you found treasure," Officer Libby Marshall commented.

"Something like it. We'll have to get all of this to the station and take a closer look."

"My place or yours?" Shriver joked.

Jordan barely refrained from glaring at him for the inappropriate joke and making things awkward when this could turn out to be a fabulous day, warrants and all.

"I think we can keep this in Homicide for now."

If Shriver had noticed her tone cooling, he didn't let it show. Libby winced.

"Fine with me," Shriver said. This will take some time to get through. We better get some coffee first."

"Suit yourself."

Jordan wouldn't mind being able to close this case quickly. That would perhaps leave enough resources for Ellie to continue her inquiries into the Wilder case. As for Shriver—at some point he had to realize that trying too hard would get him nowhere.

Much of the day was not going as Ellie had anticipated. She'd thought that after Driscoll's interrogation, she could see the niece and nephew of Stella Brown who lived on the same street, a couple of blocks from one another. Jordan had planned to contact Waters to ask to see his father...they weren't doing either one.

The lieutenant had decided she should help with looking into the McDonalds as well as Mr. Gentry some more, to see if they could find anything to back up Driscoll's story.

While she was aware of the urgency, Ellie worried that by next week, Carroll would ask her to terminate her investigation.

She was beginning to wonder if he had a point, and she had allowed herself to be distracted by a romantic notion.

When Jordan and Detective Shriver returned to the station with boxes full of documents, Ellie realized quickly that she'd need to reschedule with the Browns. She picked up the phone and called Stella Brown's niece Emily. Getting only the voice-mail, she left a message.

"This is Detective Harding. I'm really sorry, but I can't make it tonight. I'd like to reschedule. I'll get in touch soon." She wondered if they could still see Kathryn this evening. Jordan looked ready to settle in for some overtime.

Even while focused on her task, Ellie could tell that the Major Crimes detective was trying to make an impression, on the lieutenant and on Jordan.

For the rest of the afternoon, they worked side by side, going through every document line after line.

"I never thought I'd say this, but I'm beginning to think Driscoll is telling the truth—a part of it anyway," Jordan admitted. "This shows they used the store for some shady activities. Time for a closer look at the McDonalds."

"So, let's get ourselves some warrants," Shriver suggested. He took a look at his watch. "It might be a little late today."

"I saw Valerie a few minutes ago," Ellie said. "Tell me what you need, and I'll get her on the phone."

"Great idea. Basically, we need to look at bank records from the past ten to twelve years, in the time they've been doing those 'investments'," Jordan formed quotation marks with her fingers, "through the store. There might be other businesses involved, and we need a clearer picture."

"All right, I'm on it."

Back at her desk, phone in hand, Ellie smiled, a somewhat delayed reaction to Jordan's casual praise. She hoped she could live up to the more seasoned detectives' expectations.

Valerie picked up on the second ring, listening to what Ellie had to tell her.

"So, things are moving on your end? I'll see what I can do, but it's still a bit early in the game. They have their lawyers ready."

"I know, but thank you. We appreciate your help."

"Expect nothing tonight, though."

"Okay then. I'll talk to you tomorrow."

She went back to update Jordan and Shriver.

"Yeah, that's what I expected," Jordan said. "Let's call it a day? We'll get back to it first thing in the morning."

"Sounds good to me. I'll be right back," Ellie said. When she returned after a quick bathroom break, she was just in time to overhear Shriver's invitation, clearly for Jordan only.

"So, would you like to grab a bite to eat?"

"Sorry, but I have plans."

"Another time then? There's something I'd like to discuss."

Ellie cleared her throat, and Jordan gave her a half shrug.

"Another time," she said. "Have a good evening."

"Sure. I'll see you tomorrow."

"What was that all about?" Ellie asked when they were walking to her car.

"I don't know. He's okay, but I'm not that curious. Look, I know today didn't go as planned, but I don't see why we can't stop by Waters' place...You just stay in the car. Carroll didn't say how far away you had to be."

"Okay...I thought that could wait a day."

"Work first. I promised you, and Kathryn isn't going anywhere."

"Neither is Waters, but whatever works for you."

"Yeah. I'll make this quick."

⁂

"What the hell?" Waters grumbled behind the safety chain. He looked like he hadn't shaved in days, and perhaps that was true. Jordan couldn't bring herself to feel sympathy for a man who had misused and abused the power that came with his job.

"It's about a case. I need to talk to your father."

He gave a surprised laugh. "You got a lot of nerve coming here. My father? Forget about it. He retired a long time ago, and even if I was interested in helping you, chances are he couldn't tell you anything. Old man never talked much about the job, and now he forgot most of it."

That was what Jordan had feared.

"He might remember this one. Young woman got slaughtered in her dorm room, they put away the boyfriend for life...Do you remember if your dad ever talked about it?"

Waters looked puzzled at that.

"Didn't the guy die not long ago? What the fuck are you doing looking into this case now...oh wait. I know. Damn. Is she running that department now?"

Jordan suppressed a sigh. Waters might be a jerk, a criminal even, but he had been a detective for a long time.

"The family had some reasonable doubts, and Carroll okayed us looking into it."

"I don't give a flying fuck what Carroll okayed. My Dad worked his ass off on the job, and so did I. You might have smeared my reputation. You're not going to do the same to his."

"Smeared..." Those accusations made Jordan so angry she could barely breathe. She had seen this kind of attitude in serial killers, cult members, and your garden variety misogynist. It sickened her to hear it from a man she had worked with for many years.

"You did that to yourself, and you know it."

"Do I? People can't take a joke anymore."

"Oh, really? When Atwood threatened Ellie with withdrawing backup for payback, that was a joke too? For Christ's sake!"

At this moment, Jordan was angrier at herself than she was at him. She'd never meant to bring Ellie into the conversation, and she was certain this was exactly what Carroll had wanted to avoid.

"I don't know anything about that," Waters said irritably.

"Well, you do now. So, what am I going to tell the lieutenant about your dad?"

"If you want to talk to him, I'll be there too."

"Not a problem. Just let me know when."

"This Sunday, 3 p.m. When I say the conversation is over, it's over."

"Fair enough," Jordan said. "Thank you."

"Yeah, whatever."

This had been somewhat successful...except that she'd been stalling regarding Kathryn, and Ellie was well aware of it. On her way down the stairs to the lobby, Jordan called the number. Kathryn picked up right away.

"Jordan, is everything okay? It's late."

"Everybody's fine. I was wondering if I could drop by before work tomorrow."

"Of course. You know you're always welcome. You're bringing Ellie, right? I can make you breakfast."

"You don't have to."

"Please."

Jordan refrained from using Waters' parting words, "yeah, whatever." Instead, she said, "Okay. Thanks." She didn't mention that the subject she was going to raise might curb everyone's appetite. Kathryn didn't ask. "See you tomorrow then."

Jordan ended the call and opened the door to step out on the sidewalk. A few seconds later, she sat in the car next to Ellie who studied her anxiously.

"Right. You're going to be so proud of me."

Ellie was proud of Jordan indeed, because she knew that every contact with Kathryn held underlying tension.

She had shown her appreciation in verbal and non-verbal ways, and even offered to, once again, stay in the car if necessary.

"She might be more open if it's just between the two of you."

"Perhaps, but I'll take the risk."

The time for stalling had come and gone, as they went to visit Kathryn in her home for the first time since the last conflict that had resulted in her and her husband being uninvited from the wedding. Jordan had talked to her biological mother since, but not seen her at her place.

The smell of coffee and pastries seemed odd given the kind of conversation they were going to have. At the same time, Ellie appreciated Kathryn's attempt to have a relationship with her daughter, however stressed at times. Jordan's smile was further reassurance. Perhaps they could do this quick, with the necessary caution, no one getting hurt. The story already held too much pain for these two women.

"Well...good morning. Thanks for having us," Jordan began.

Jim, Kathryn's husband, had said hello to them, but left soon after.

"I'm happy to. How are you doing? I'm really glad you caught this Morgan person. That's crazy, pretending to be someone's relative. I'm sorry, Ellie." Kathryn's rambling showed her nervousness.

"It's okay," Ellie was quick to say. "Thank you. We're fine now." This wasn't about her.

"Yeah. There's really no good way to say this, and I apologize in advance, but I need to know something." Jordan looked at the croissant on her plate as if wondering if she'd still feel like having food a minute from now. "You once told me you had a miscarriage before you had me."

Kathryn looked more perplexed than hurt.

"I meant to ask you if that's something that runs in the family. If you know."

All kinds of conflicting emotions chased one another in Kathryn's expression, as she was probably making the connection.

"Are you...?"

"No. Not yet. We are planning to."

Joy about the news won over everything else.

"That is wonderful! I am so happy for you."

Ellie sensed that she wanted to get up to hug Jordan, but she opted for taking Jordan's hands, for a brief moment.

"Thank you. So?"

Kathryn sat back. Perhaps, she, too, was stalling.

"My mother never said anything, so I'm afraid I don't know. Someone might have mentioned it if there had been a history? It happened very early, and then, when I had you, there was no problem, so I think you'll be okay. This is so amazing."

"Yes. It is. And thank you. I know this can't be easy for you."

"I'm happy to help, but please, eat."

Ellie couldn't help thinking that something deeply important had just happened, and she was happy to witness it.

❦

While the team was still working on unraveling more of the complicated strings behind the McDonalds' operations, Ellie left to meet with Emily Brown, Stella's niece. Her brother Stephen who lived down the street with his family, was present as well.

No cookies this time.

"I'm not sure what this is going to achieve, after all these years," Emily opened the conversation. "And honestly? I'm glad that he's finally died. It took too damn long."

"Em. You might not want to talk like this in front of the police," Stephen reminded her.

"Why not? I didn't kill him, and I don't know who did. Besides, I don't think this young woman is saddened that a monster is gone."

This was not going to be easy, Ellie reflected. But she hadn't chosen this job for "easy."

"There was never a doubt for any of you that George Wilder murdered your aunt?"

"I wasn't born yet, and Emily was too young to understand what happened at the time," Stephen admitted, "but our mother talked about it a lot. She and Stella were close."

"That's a polite way of phrasing it," Emily scoffed. "The truth is it killed her too. She died in a car accident, at least that's what the police said. I always thought she meant to drive the car off the bridge."

"I'm so sorry."

"Why are you here anyway, after all this time?"

"There have been some questions around...George Wilder's guilt."

"You can't be serious. That's what you spend my taxpayer's dollars on? You have nothing better to do?"

"Mr. Wilder's family raised some concerns that we need to take seriously."

"Well, yeah, Mrs. Byrd has always told a different kind of story. Wouldn't you, if a close relative of yours was accused of murder? According to Mom, she was away in college for most of the time. Aunt Stella was very smart, and she had big plans, that might have not included him. He got angry. Happens a lot, doesn't it?"

Ellie had to admit it happened more often than she would have liked.

"Do you know Mrs. Montgomery?"

"She's an odd lady," Emily said instantly, her brother's expression indicating that he wasn't happy with her comment. Emily ignored him. "She's always been strange, as long as I know her. At first, she believed he was guilty, but for decades, she visits him in prison once, twice a month. Who does that?"

"I think she, too, changed her mind."

"I wouldn't know why…They found a bloody axe wrapped in a Goddamn bloody shirt of his. My grandparents had to identify her. What do you think that did to our family?"

"Again, I'm sorry. I won't bother you for long. Just one more question—Stella, George and Enid Montgomery spent a lot of time together, didn't they?"

"Not according to our mother. Enid, Mrs. Montgomery, was tagging along sometimes, but Stella was popular, and by association, George Wilder was too. You know what they say about the fifth wheel."

"So, she was jealous?"

"I said she was weird. I can't speak to anything else. He's dead, my aunt is, why not give it a rest? Enid might have been a bit jealous, but she also admired Stella. And she's what, almost eighty now? I wish you'd leave it alone. It's not like she murdered Stella. This is upsetting for all of us, and don't you think we deserve closure?"

"I do. Thank you so much for talking to me," Ellie said.

This conversation had done nothing to disperse the idea that Enid and Stella might have been more involved than anyone had thought. It also didn't shake Wilder's conviction.

She didn't drive to the *Night Shift*, where she was supposed to meet Jordan, right away, but stopped at Enid Montgomery's.

"Oh dear, you're back," the older woman said. "That's wonderful." She was leaning heavily on her cane.

"I'm sorry to disturb you."

"Oh no, you're not. Can I offer you something? A sherry maybe?"

"No, thanks."

"Please, sit down."

"I won't stay long," Ellie said, wondering how she could approach the subject in a diplomatic way. "I came from Stella's family."

"Those poor things. They never sought solace in forgiveness, I guess."

"You told me you and Stella were good friends."

"Of course. Did they say otherwise?"

At this point, Ellie was beginning to see the futility in trying to get people to remember events from sixty years ago.

"Not exactly. I was wondering...Was there ever anything between you and Stella that George might have been misinterpreted?"

Enid Montgomery gave her a quizzical look. "What do you mean, dear?"

"Or maybe he didn't have it wrong. I'm not judging—I just want to know the truth. George might have been angry at both you and Stella for—"

"For what?" For the first time since Ellie met her, Enid was angry. She practically spat the words. "What are you saying, that I had unnatural relations with Stella? That's nasty of you to think! I thought you were trying to help Doreen, not smearing anyone's good name..."

"I'm sorry I misunderstood," Ellie said, her skin crawling all of a sudden. She hadn't expected the nice elderly lady from her last visit to turn into a raging homophobe within seconds. She could be more than that. A murderer. Or maybe Natalie, who so easily slipped from one persona to the other as well, had made her paranoid. Not every bigot was a murderer, were they?

She waited a few heartbeats, but Ms. Montgomery made no attempt to correct the statement made in her outburst.

"I'll go now."

"You do that. You can come back but never ask me things like that again. I'm sad that a bright young lady like you would even think of this."

Ellie chose not to answer.

⁂

Waiting for Ellie at the *Night Shift*, Jordan had started on a salad and a glass of water with a slice of lemon. When Ellie arrived and a waitress appeared at the table almost immediately, she ordered a sandwich and a beer.

"You look like you've seen a ghost," Jordan commented. "What happened?"

"I'm starting to believe I'm chasing one. But that's not the reason. I asked—in a very subtle way—if Enid might have been attracted to Stella, or if anyone might have thought she was. You should have been there. That transformation was something. Turns out she's a gay-hating bigot."

"She threatened you?" Jordan hadn't met Montgomery, but she didn't consider age an excuse for a person to unleash their prejudice on her wife—or anyone.

"Not in so many words, but it's a good thing she didn't know anything about me before she offered me cookies. I'd be afraid of what's in them." With a sigh, Ellie leaned back into the booth, taking a sip of her beer. Jordan didn't blame her for suspending the "no alcohol" rule for herself.

"You could be on to something," she offered.

"It's easy to manipulate memories and expectations," Ellie said darkly. "Maybe he did it. Maybe she did. Or they did it together, hell if I know."

"A lot of people seem to be acting strange. To me, it sounds like you're on to something."

"We'll see. Thank you for dealing with Waters on a Sunday."

Jordan shrugged. "I don't think it's going to be long."

They were both silent for a moment long enough for Jordan's thoughts to wander to tomorrow's appointment. Kathryn hadn't answered all her questions, but she had given them as much reassurance as she possibly could. They were going forward.

Part of her wondered why Kathryn had never sought her family's help, even after the second pregnancy as a teenager. Kathryn had told her she didn't know how to ask for help, but sometimes, her biological mother had created diversions and smokescreens even when she didn't mean to—this could be such a time.

"You thought about when you're going to tell the lieutenant?"

"Well, not before there is something to tell him."

Ellie laughed a little, well aware that she was getting ahead of herself. "There will be soon."

"Hey. So, this is real," Casey, who had stopped at their table, commented. "I haven't seen you have a drink in weeks. When's the happy occasion?"

"We're still prepping for it," Jordan said. "But don't tell anyone yet. Ellie's looking at colleges for the kid, but I'd prefer we start talking to people when there's actually a reason."

"My lips are sealed," Casey promised. She pulled herself a chair. "Don't worry, it will be fine. There's a protocol in place. I wasn't a fan of light duty, but that time goes by at some point. College is a bit early, but you might want to start looking into daycare soon, if that's something you'll need. Long waiting lists are not unusual."

"Wow. Would you be willing to come over for dinner sometime, so we can take notes?"

"Sure." Casey laughed. "You'll figure it out."

Strangely enough, Jordan was certain that they would. For once.

Chapter Seven

S he wasn't as certain regarding her meeting with Waters' father, but this was probably Ellie's last chance to keep the case going. Carroll had postponed the briefing to Monday, and Jordan was determined to give it her best shot.

She found it hard not to get distracted when she met Cliff Waters in the parking lot of the facility. He had always come across as someone prejudiced. When she first met him, she thought that she—and other colleagues—could live with that as long as he focused on getting the job done. At the end, his motivation had waned, revealing an uglier picture. Even now, he was radiating self-righteous anger because of a crisis of his own making. It made her *angry*—at herself, because she couldn't help thinking they should have done something before he turned to assault.

"Remember, I'll be the one talking," he warned her.

"I remember. It was only a couple of days ago."

Waters senior had been a cop. His son was a disgraced cop. When Cliff Waters talked to a woman at the reception desk, Jordan studied the surroundings. There was a huge park behind the five-story building. Inside, it was all shiny and clean materials, staff milling about, patients well taken care of. This kind of care didn't come cheap. She could come up with a few theories, none of them reassuring, but that wasn't the job today. She needed to find out if Joseph Waters knew anything about the Wilder case.

Waters' father was sitting on a bench on the terrace.

"Hey Dad."

A smile lit up the older man's face.

"I didn't know you were coming today."

"Something came up. I promise we won't bother you for long."

It came to Jordan's mind that this wasn't at all what the older Waters had meant.

"This is Detective Carpenter, a colleague of mine. They, we," he caught himself, "are looking into an old case of yours. George Wilder?"

He hesitated, and Jordan was afraid Cliff Waters might be right, and his father didn't remember much about his work.

"There was a story about it on TV recently," Cliff prompted.

"Oh yes, of course. Wilder! Jesus, how much time do you have? You should get yourself a coffee and sit down for a bit." He winked at Jordan. "These days it can take me a little longer to gather my thoughts, but it's all still up there," he said, tapping his temple with a finger.

"She doesn't have much time."

"Oh no, she's fine," Jordan said. "Please, take the time you need."

"You heard the lady. Cliff, why don't you get us all a coffee?"

Cliff Waters looked like he wanted to protest, but then he got up and walked away. If Jordan had wanted to use the time to tell his father that they weren't colleagues any longer, she wouldn't have managed. Waters returned only a moment later, and someone from the kitchen staff followed behind with a tray.

"You came to the Wilder case a little later," Jordan began, earning a warning glance from her *former* colleague.

"That's right. One of the guys was on leave, and I joined Riley. Not that there was much to do for me. They had a pretty iron-clad case. It went to trial quick, and Wilder was convicted."

"Did ever have any doubt about his guilt?"

"Didn't you hear what he just said?" Waters muttered.

"Frankly? It seemed a little too easy, but it was hard to argue with the evidence. A bloody axe. Wilder's family paid for some additional testing, later, when it was available, but the blood was the victim's, and there was no evidence suggesting the presence of another party."

"Did you have any other suspects?"

"We looked at some of the other friends, but Wilder was the boyfriend, he had means and opportunity, and let's face it, no one could see the girl's girlfriends wielding that axe."

"Unless she was subdued somehow. Both she and George had been drinking that night."

"A possibility, if a far-fetched one."

"I think that's enough now," Waters interrupted.

"Come on. I never get to meet someone who wants to pick my brain for a case anymore. I'm quite enjoying this."

"Thank you, Mr. Waters." This wasn't the turn of events Jordan had expected, but she could work with it. "Is there anything else you remember? Anything that struck you as odd?"

He gave this some thought.

"There was this woman who came to trial every day. She said she was a friend of Stella Brown's, but none of the other kids really confirmed that. At first, we thought she wanted to see him go to prison, but she went to visit him a lot later."

Homophobic Ms. Montgomery. But that didn't necessarily mean anything in this context.

"She had an alibi?"

"A bit sketchy, studying at home. Some other students saw her, but not all of the time. However, we believed her, and remember, the evidence was damning."

"Yes. Mr. Waters, thank you so much."

"My pleasure, Detective. Have a good day."

Jordan hadn't expected Waters to thank her for not telling his father, and he didn't. Obviously, that was his business, though she was surprised at finding that Waters senior seemed like a decent man. Aside from that, unfortunately, there wasn't much she could tell Ellie to help her case.

❦

The future was looking exciting after the appointment they'd been anticipating for a while now...her venture into the past, not so much, Ellie thought when she knocked on Jill Allen's door. To her surprise, she heard the laughter of a young child. This might be yet another sign to let go of said past. Jill opened the door to her, wearing jeans and a t-shirt with slippers.

"Hi, Ellie. Please, excuse the mess. I couldn't get the babysitter today. Fortunately, my boss is flexible about letting me work from home. I take it you have news?"

"Unfortunately." Ellie gingerly stepped over a cluster of building blocks to follow Jill into the living room where a little girl was sitting on the floor, playing with more blocks. She was about two, three years old.

"I really tried," she said. "I spoke to everyone I could find that still had a connection to the case. Most of them were convinced Wilder did it, and those who weren't, didn't have the evidence to back up their doubts. Enid Montgomery visited him many times over the years, and there are a few people who have expressed unease with her. Well, she made me uneasy, but of course that's not enough to suggest she murdered anyone."

"You did everything you could. So did I. It is strange that everything seems to lead back to Montgomery."

"Yeah. She seems to have created her own reality."

With a glance at her child, Jill sighed. "We hit a wall, didn't we? I believe Mrs. Byrd. You met her. She isn't misguided. Other people had doubts, and I think that matters. I want my child to grow up in a world where she can still have faith in the justice system, however hard that can be these days."

That was something Ellie could relate to more than ever before.

"Things have to get better at some point. We are working towards it."

"Yes, but are we succeeding? Things around us just seem to get worse. Even I don't know anymore if I should keep going with this, when so much else is happening in the present."

"It's true. I'll have to talk to the lieutenant, see what he says. If he and the A.D.A. think it's over, I'm afraid it is."

Ellie wasn't happy with this solution, but she had to admit that Jill had a point. The past few weeks had been fraught with personal issues alongside with the job, Natalie and the aftermath. If—when, she corrected herself—Jordan was pregnant, it would be the same, just for a happier reason.

At some point, things wouldn't be so quiet at work.

Maybe, Doreen Byrd would understand that no investigation would bring her brother back. Maybe it would be enough for her that someone had taken her seriously...Still, the thought that Stella Brown's killer might have been never found, bothered Ellie. It didn't matter how long ago it happened. A woman had been brutally murdered.

She couldn't let it go.

Ellie left Jill Allen's apartment with the promise to update her soon. Lost in thought, she walked to her car, parked a block away. Had she done her part to get justice for Doreen? Stella Brown or George Wilder? She honestly wasn't sure. Neither seemed Waters senior to be, though Detective Riley had pretty much blown her off. Doubts remained, but that was all she could unearth from the past—doubts.

It took her a few seconds to realize that the footsteps she heard had been following her, closer now. A stranger crowding her never failed to bring up particular, uncomfortable memories, but she was quite sure that this wasn't a stranger.

Fellow police officer Chris Atwood had recently threatened her over testifying against Cliff Waters. Carroll had reined him in, but Atwood still resented her, she knew. He had even accused her of sleeping her way into the detective's job.

"Chris, give it a rest," she muttered, spinning around a few feet from her car.

The man in his forties certainly wasn't Atwood or any of his friends.

"Detective Ellie Harding?" he asked.

<hr>

Jordan had been feeling restless all day. Her case had taken a bizarre turn. She had helped Ellie with hers best she could. Perhaps it was the 24/7 news cycle she couldn't escape, even when at work. Ellie was still working. If she went to the *Night Shift*, she'd find some familiar faces for sure, but even there would be a TV on.

She could see her parents, though she and Ellie had decided they would talk to them together once there was something exciting to talk about.

Derek had texted her, asking if the opening of the new and improved *Code 7* was imminent. She had assured him he wouldn't miss anything.

That left...Without thinking, Jordan took the exit that would take her to the one place she had avoided for some time, except for the one occasion that had almost turned into an interrogation—if it wasn't for Ellie. She was on her own now, and for some unfathomable reason, she had the urge to see Kathryn.

She and Jim had finished dinner when Jordan arrived, exchanging a surprised look. That was to be expected. In the past Jordan hadn't come by often when it wasn't about police business.

"I was putting away leftovers, but everything is still warm if you like," Kathryn offered.

"No, thank you. I just wanted to..." Talk? She'd been here not long ago. What else was there to say?

Kathryn cast another look at her husband before she said, "Why don't we take a walk then?"

"Sure. Thank you."

"No problem."

Being around Jim would be awkward given their shared history, but even more so since Jordan had found out that he wasn't her biological father. TJ Pratt—an unpleasant story she didn't want to think about at the moment.

When they had walked a few steps, Kathryn spoke. "Don't get me wrong, I'm happy to see you. I always am—but this is twice in a few days. Is everything okay?"

Jordan laughed wryly. "Do you watch the news? Nothing is okay. Well, Ellie and I are. We should know in a few weeks if we are pregnant." If she said "we," perhaps she'd be less anxious about the idea? It worked somewhat.

"That's amazing. I'm happy for you," Kathryn said, her tone guarded. That, Jordan assumed, was in response to her jibe.

"I've been following the news some, but it's hard. All those children separated from their parents. Some might never see each other again."

If she was honest, Jordan had known that she'd say something like that. She couldn't deny Kathryn her feelings, but back in those days when CPS came around, their actions weren't unfair. Kathryn and Jim had broken the law to get to that point. There was no way to compare their circumstances to those of parents fleeing violence. If she had known all of this, why did she come here? Kathryn seemed to wonder as well.

"I missed you. I really did, even when I got to live with Jack and Pauline."

"I missed you too. So much."

"I wasn't sure you'd notice I was gone." And she'd felt guilty every time she'd had those thoughts. "I thought you should know."

"Thank you."

"And I wanted to say it before I'll have a child who will want to know about their grandparents." This was dangerous territory, but if anything, she wasn't a coward.

"You'd be okay with me being in your child's life?"

"I think I owe it to them."

It was the first time she wasn't caught off guard by Kathryn's spontaneous hug, the first time she didn't feel the urge to step away. Whatever issues she had, and would always have with her, she'd still give her daughter or son every possible option.

Kathryn was well aware of what she'd said—Jordan didn't owe *her*. Even now, the peace between them was precarious. It didn't mean she could afford to go to a place where she'd have to admit she needed Kathryn in her life. Not because Pauline or Jack would mind.

They had come to a slightly rackety bench at the end of the clearing.

"Let's sit for a moment," Kathryn said. "There's something you should know."

"I'm not sure I like the sound of that."

"I want you to know that I tried. To ask for help. Yes, I said otherwise, but I guess I couldn't bear to remember, and I didn't want you to get the wrong idea. I shouldn't have kept any of it from you, and I'm sorry." Kathryn's words came stumbling out before Jordan had time to put her guard back in place.

"My parents cut me off, completely. They didn't even talk to me after I went to live with Jim. I sent them pictures of you, hoping it would change their minds, do something."

"But it didn't," Jordan concluded. "Are they still alive?" Even if they were, she wasn't sure what she'd do with that kind of information.

"No. They sent my brother down here to tell me to never contact them again. That I was dead to them. That's when things got really bad." When Jordan didn't answer, still absorbing what she'd heard, Kathryn added, "It's not an excuse. I thought you deserved to know—and that it would mean the world to me if I can see the baby."

"Yes. Thank you. You know I think Ellie must be off work by now."

There was no such thing as having a simple conversation with her biological mother. If she was honest, Jordan had always imagined the story had been something like this. She didn't need confirmation that there was more family out there, family that had turned their backs on a young mother and a baby...She and Ellie would do better. That was the only lesson she wanted to take from this.

Chapter Eight

The man didn't waste any time explaining himself to Ellie.

"I'll leave you alone in a minute, but I need you to do something for me," he said. "Stop bothering Enid. I don't know what you're hoping to accomplish, but it's not good for her. She gets confused when people press her about the past."

"And you are?" Ellie asked, cautiously still keeping her hand close to her gun. He might have honest intentions but walking up to her like this was still odd. One time, she hadn't paid attention, and it had cost her.

"I'm Jamie Ryan, her grandnephew. I take care of her. Enid is my grandfather's sister. My parents died when I was young, so she took care of me. She's the only family I have left."

"I'm sorry about your parents." Ellie truly was, though she still didn't understand what he was trying to tell her. "That was kind of her."

"It was. And I don't like people harassing her."

"I wasn't. Look...Why don't we sit down and talk about it?" Ellie pointed to the diner across the street. "I understand Enid was friends with both the victim and the accused. I was just asking her some questions, to which she didn't object."

He reluctantly walked with her.

"It might not seem that way to you, but she's not in such good health anymore. She tries to ignore it, but there are times when she lives in the past more than the present, and frankly, you didn't help."

"I'm sorry about that."

Ellie was still baffled. Enid didn't seem confused during their conversations about her past experiences, or her, however misguided, views.

They walked inside the diner where they sat down, and both ordered a coffee. The smell of food made her hungry, but she still had hope she could have dinner with Jordan later.

"Did she say anything to you? About the case?"

"Sometimes, she talks as if it happened weeks ago. Remember, she lost a friend, and another turned out to be a murderer. You brought up many traumatic memories, and for what? Wilder is dead."

"Yes, I'm aware. But Enid kept those memories alive by visiting him on a regular basis."

He ripped the small packet of sugar open, emptying it into his coffee, then reached for another one.

"She has a good heart. People are bound to take advantage, and believe me, they have taken advantage of her for a long time."

"Are you talking about Stella? Or George Wilder?"

"Maybe. She felt guilty for a long time, for no reason. There is nothing new to uncover—Wilder killed his girlfriend, he went to prison. End of story."

"Enid is lucky to have you."

"I was lucky to have her," he insisted. "Without her, I don't know what would have happened."

74

Ryan's passionate defense was still on Ellie's mind when she walked through the door of the *Night Shift*, looking for Jordan. As she walked past the hallway leading to the restrooms, she vaguely noticed the two women sharing a passionate kiss. Ellie felt her jaw drop when she recognized both of them, but she managed to hurry past before either of them could recognize her.

Jordan sat alone at the bar, nursing a ginger ale.

"Hey." Ellie kissed her in greeting before she sat on the barstool next to her. "You come here often?"

With the joke, she managed to draw Jordan out of what seemed to be a pensive mood.

Jordan laughed. "Are you trying to pick me up?"

"Well, I already know you're going home with me. How was your day?"

In the mood for something sweet, Ellie ordered a Virgin Piña Colada.

"Probably a lot more boring that yours. I've been here a while."

"Yeah, about that, I'm sorry, but I had an interesting conversation with Enid Montgomery's grandnephew."

"Really? Where did he come from?"

"His parents died young, so Enid took him in. He seems to be very loyal. He also told me to stay away from her."

Jordan sat up straighter. "He threatened you?"

Having expected her reaction, Ellie hurried to explain. "We had a fairly amicable conversation over coffee. I'm not sure what to think about him yet, but Enid sure is full of surprises. I'd like to look into him."

"To be honest, I'm not sure what that's going to achieve. He's too young to know anything about the case."

"He knows about Enid. That is of interest to me," Ellie insisted. "So, what about your boring day?"

"I went to push Kathryn a bit regarding family secrets," Jordan admitted.

"Oh. How did that go?"

"No too badly." Jordan picked up her glass, swirling the carbonated drink. "In fact, that wasn't even the point. There are so many children who live with uncertainty and fear, I don't want ours to ever feel that way. They will know that they belong and will be cared for."

"Of course." Ellie wasn't sure she understood the whole scope of the conversation yet, theirs, or the one Jordan had with Kathryn earlier.

"Well, that part was surprisingly easy. I also learned a bit more about her family, and it turns out I have an uncle. Cousins maybe, we didn't get there, because I sort of bailed."

"That's a lot already, I imagine. Do you want to meet them?"

"I thought about it," Jordan said. "No. I think it's enough, Kathryn trying to make amends, Pratt in prison, and...these nice folks who apparently kicked a pregnant teenage girl out on the street and cut all ties. It seems that she tried after the second pregnancy, sending them baby pictures and all. In return, they sent her brother to threaten her. She really had no one to turn to."

Ellie wanted to say something, but she suppressed the impulse, knowing that Jordan had long come to the same conclusion.

"And no, it's not an excuse, but in any case, that makes it easier to draw the line. She really wants to be in the baby's life, and I don't see a reason to deny her that. Other than that, we'll be taking it easy where the extended family is concerned."

"Sounds like a good plan."

It made Ellie ridiculously happy that they were talking about "the baby" now as if that was already reality. It would be. Not long from now.

Two days later, Ellie couldn't stall Lieutenant Carroll any longer. He and A.D.A. Esposito called the investigation officially closed. Ellie couldn't blame them. She hadn't brought them reasonable doubt that Wilder had not killed Stella Brown—a crime of passion, or cold blood, they might never know the details. Wilder could have told the truth, or he could have been a psychopath who had fooled his family and friends. As for Enid, Jamie would be happy that there was no reason for Ellie to go back. Not that she was much inclined to see the woman again.

Ellie noticed that A.D.A. Esposito shared a smile with Maria Doss before she left the station after the briefing. The memory of the kiss between the two women was still on Ellie's mind. A little bit of gossip she had yet to share with Jordan, though at the moment, she didn't feel much like it. She couldn't put her finger on it...but that was the problem, right? The Wilder case was unlike anything she'd ever seen in her job. So much information unavailable that these days, they relied on—and, on getting it quick. For a moment, she wondered if exhumation of Stella Brown's body was a realistic idea, or something out of the movies, and what it could do anyway.

She opened the file again. Jamie Ryan had a record, and it wasn't about youthful misdemeanors. Domestic disputes, bar brawls and the likes. When he'd told his story, he made it look like his problems had started after his parents' death, around the time Enid took him in—but those reports were from much later. Enid kept paying for lawyers. No surprise he felt indebted to her. There was something there...but she hadn't succeeded in solving the mystery. It might remain one forever.

"Hey, why so gloomy?"

Ellie jumped to her feet at the sound of a familiar voice and accepted a quick hug from Derek Henderson whose mood seemed the opposite of her own.

"Hi, welcome back. We missed you. Some of us mostly because they had to get their own coffee," she said, referring to Maria Doss's comments about Derek's frequent coffee runs.

Maria shook her head. "She was not supposed to tell you that. How was the camping?"

"It was...camping," Derek said. "We might look into something with solid walls and a roof next time."

"I knew it." Maria went back to her work with a triumphant smile on her face.

"So, what else is new? Where's my partner?"

"You're going to see her in a bit." Everyone turned around at the sounds of the lieutenant's voice. Carroll looked serious.

"Welcome back, Henderson. We have a dead body at the Capitol Inn. Carpenter's on her way. Harding, I want you to go as well. Major Crimes will be on the scene, so try not to step on anyone's toes."

"Major Crimes, why?" Derek asked.

Ellie was curious too.

"Apparently, there's an overlap with another of their cases. Carpenter and Shriver will fill you in."

"All right. Ellie?"

She was already waiting, keys in hand.

❦

The businessman who'd been found dead by the room maid had checked into the hotel room under a false name. That in itself was curious. Jordan was aware of Shriver's gaze on her as she studied the body. One shot to the chest—whoever had killed Marius Callum, was not an amateur. They had yet to analyze the security footage. Callum didn't have a record at a first quick check, but the letter from McDonald Ltd and their business card had brought Major Crimes onto the scene.

While the homicide investigation on the convenience store murders was closed, Major Crimes was still working on un-raveling the many threads of the McDonalds' reach beyond the money laundering—or so Shriver had told her. He'd also promised to keep her in the loop if they discovered anything relevant to her job, and here they were again.

Jordan had a headache. She thought it was quite unfair given that all she'd had to drink the previous night was ginger ale and a sip of Ellie's non-alcoholic Piña Colada. There was not enough caffeine in the world now—what would it be like to cut it completely?

"I suppose you're going to pay the McDonalds a visit in prison?"

"More like a walk of shame all the way to their mansion," Shriver said. "Unless we can prove they were involved in this shooting."

"Really? What happened?"

He shrugged. "Ridiculously low bail...excellent lawyers that keep stalling...You know what it's like. They didn't pull the trig-ger on your victims in the store, and as for Driscoll...he doesn't have that kind of lawyers. McKenzie got him the best deal he could get, but the story's still shaky."

"I hate loose ends," she said with emphasis. "That and enti-tled criminals."

"But we always get them in the end, don't we?"

"Derek Henderson, thank God! You did bring me coffee, didn't you?"

"You too?" he asked, feigning hurt.

Detective Shriver was studying the exchange with interest.

"I'm joking! I'm glad you're here. I could use some caffeine though." She was surprised to see Ellie coming in after Derek, not looking too happy. That meant her investigation of the Wilder case had come to an end. Jordan couldn't help but agree with the lieutenant. A businessman found dead in one of the most expensive hotels in the city was bound to create some pressure from higher ups. Obviously, this case was more pressing than a sixty-year-old case ending in a conviction.

Dr. Adams gave Derek a wistful look, that, Jordan assumed, had little to do with anything job-related.

"It's getting a little crowded in here," she said. "How soon can we move him?"

"That's something I would like to know."

The hotel manager had arrived with Officer Potts. "I hate to be cynical, but this is already costing me. The sooner you can wrap this up, the better. You can use the conference room on the third floor. There's coffee." Seeing the detectives exchange surprised looks, she added, "Any incentive I can give you to get you and the dead body out of here."

<hr />

She had also provided them with the security footage—it showed Mr. Callum leaving his room shortly before 10 p.m. and returning half an hour later. No one else showed up on the video. The manager confirmed that the two rooms closest to Callum's hadn't been rented out, the other guests on the same floor had already checked out earlier this week.

"There was something though..." She remembered. "We had a booking for the room next to his, but they canceled at the last minute. Well, not so last minute that they had to pay."

For a brief moment, Jordan had hope. A paper trail. "Even if they canceled, they would have to give a credit card number. We're going to need that information."

The manager could have asked for a warrant, but she didn't. "Give me a moment."

"So," Derek said when she was out of earshot. "You did some interdepartmental collaboration while I was away."

Jordan followed his gaze to where Noah Shriver was standing in the corner, on the phone with either his boss or the McDonalds' lawyer. Ellie was with the officers that had been talking to hotel guests.

"He's all right."

"You're not looking for a change, are you?"

"Are you jealous?" she asked, amused. "Put your mind at ease, I think he's the one looking for a change. He keeps dropping hints, but so far, we've been interrupted by new developments on the case...or now, cases. I think he has his eyes set on Homicide."

"Homicide or one detective in particular?"

Jordan shook her head. "This conversation is getting completely bizarre. Let's focus on who shot Mr. Callum here."

Shriver was coming over to them, slipping his cell phone into the pocket of his jeans. "The McDonalds agreed to an interview with their lawyer present. I'm going over there now. Want to come?"

It wasn't the first time he had made an invitation to Jordan only, which hadn't gone unnoticed with her, or her partner.

Chapter Nine

"We agreed to this interview only so you'll leave us alone until that sham of a trial we're waiting for."

The lawyer cleared his throat, and Mrs. McDonald seemed to barely refrain from rolling her eyes.

Jordan sat across from the couple while Shriver remained standing on the side of the couch. It was ridiculous, she thought, that they were sitting in the couple's living room, surrounded by proof of their expensive tastes. They had tried to frame a man for a double murder. Shriver had already contacted the FBI. The McDonalds were allegedly involved in international money laundering schemes. They shouldn't be here.

"How did you know Mr. Callum?" she asked.

"Not very well," Mr. McDonald said after a nod from the lawyer. "He had done business with one of our partners, and he owed them money. He was hoping to come to an agreement, but given our situation, we couldn't help him much. That's why we wrote him."

"You didn't meet with him recently?"

"No."

"Did he contact you after the letter? With a counteroffer, maybe?" Shriver asked.

"He asked, we said no," Mrs. McDonald said. "This was the only interaction we've had. Frankly, you're wasting your time. And ours."

Jordan could sense Shriver's impatience, though she had to admit the woman had a point. If the McDonalds' crimes were in any way connected to the murder, they wouldn't find out right here and now. Neither of them would slip up in the presence of their lawyer who had probably given them a quick coaching.

"Well, thank you anyway," she said, getting to her feet. "We'll be in touch,"

"I'm sure they are involved somehow," Shriver asserted when they were back in the car. "We keep finding new documents, and the paperwork is just multiplying."

"Yeah. Seems like it will be tough to get to them."

He didn't argue. "About that conversation we had the other day...You think there might be an opening in Homicide?"

"You would have to ask the lieutenant about that. Waters was always going to retire this year, and we had a new hire, but of course it's not up to me."

"They say you and Henderson have a lot of sway with the boss. Maybe you could put in a good word for me?"

"You seem in a hurry."

"I don't want to miss my shot."

It occurred to her, all of a sudden, that she'd be on light duty for a while, and then on maternity leave. Would it be easier for Carroll to hire someone full-time, would the budget allow that, and how would her return to full-time employment work? The moment when she had to fill him in might come sooner than later.

Truth be told, she'd thought things had been great, with Ellie making herself at home, and Waters being gone. Jordan wasn't sure she was ready for more changes, but as she'd said, none of this was up to her.

Shriver was eager, that much was for sure, and so far, he had been fairly easy to work with. Perhaps there was an opportunity for all of them.

"What's wrong with Major Crimes?"

Given that this unit was run by a very capable—and female—supervisor, Jordan wanted to check a few boxes before she put in a good word for anyone.

"It has nothing to do with the people there, especially not Daniels. She knows her job. I'm just ready for a change."

"All right then. Talk to the lieutenant. He'll tell you about your options."

And she was going to tell Derek, later, that he got it wrong.

⁂

Jordan suppressed a curse at the familiar pain, telling her without a doubt that her and Ellie's plans had not worked out, at least not this time. That meant starting all over again. More of the waiting game. What was even worse, she was being caught off guard like a teenager not yet accustomed to one of the less pleasant realities of adulthood. At least the briefing was over, and Shriver had returned to his own precinct to talk to his boss.

Ellie's bag hung over her chair, but she really didn't want to be seen raiding her wife's purse. She didn't want to talk to Ellie right now but guard the disappointment for herself a little bit longer, try to come up with the right words.

No. Not this time.

There was always a next time.

Fortunately, Maria Doss was still at her desk, probably her best option at the moment.

"Hey."

"Hey...?" Maria kept her eyes on the screen but swiveled her chair around when a few seconds had passed without either of them saying anything.

"I was hoping you could help me out." Jordan dropped her voice to a whisper. This was uncomfortable enough.

"Female emergency?" Maria guessed, opening her top drawer. "Help yourself."

"Wow. All stocked up," Jordan said, glad Maria had kept her voice down as well.

"You never know. Besides, they keep the boys out of my things."

"Thanks. You're a lifesaver."

On her way back to her desk, Jordan made a beeline for the break room to get coffee and a chocolate bar. Now, to break the news to Ellie next. On the bright side, they hadn't told Jack and Pauline about their plans yet. They'd be the last people on earth to judge, Jordan knew, but somehow, that didn't make her feel better.

⁂

Jordan had rehearsed for the moment when she had to tell Ellie the news. In her mind, it was supposed to be a calm and rational conversation regarding the facts, statistics, and their options. The setting had to be right, so she texted Ellie and suggested they'd drive together after work and grab a bite to eat on the way.

So far, so good.

Ellie didn't seem to suspect anything when she got into the car, and they kissed for a greeting.

"Giovanna's?" Jordan suggested. "I had a craving for tiramisu."

"Sounds great. Is anyone else coming?"

"No, not tonight. I'd like to spend an evening alone with my wife for once." She managed a smile. Ellie laughed.

"No argument from me."

Giovanna's was often packed even during a weeknight, but they still had room to seat them, to Jordan's relief, in a fairly quiet corner hidden by a huge potted plant. All of a sudden, the secret seemed to weigh on her, more heavily than she'd imagined.

"Okay, I didn't mean to keep this from you, but I didn't want to talk about it at work. Looks like I'm not pregnant." She laughed wryly. "Forget what I said. I'm definitely not pregnant."

"Oh. Okay."

Jordan listened carefully for any signs of disappointment and sadness, but so far, they were doing well staying neutral. This was why she had wanted to do this in a public place, so she could be sure to keep her own emotions in check for this conversation.

The waitress arrived before Ellie could give her more of an answer, and they ordered.

After the young woman had left with the menus, Ellie said, "I'm so sorry. I think it's okay for us to take a moment, and...You want to try again?"

It was a valid question. There wasn't only a time limit on the general concept. Every attempt came with a substantial investment.

"I want to."

She was also scared. Of feeling like she'd failed. Of how she was going to handle that emotion.

"You know I'm with you whatever you decide." Ellie's tone was still calm as she took Jordan's hands, though her eyes had become suspiciously bright. "And whatever you might think, this is not your fault. It sucks, but it happens to a lot of people. We'll try again when the doc says it's okay."

"Another thing I found out today is that Maria keeps a giant supply of female hygiene products in her desk drawer. In case you ever have an emergency..." Jordan could think of many other things she wanted to tell Ellie that moment, but each of them had the potential to undo her carefully built guard.

"That's good to know. I love you too, more than you can ever imagine. If anything, I'm a little mad at you that you had to do this here, so we'll have to postpone a good cry."

"Don't be mad, please. It's Giovanna's, and I'll pay."

"You're right. I have nothing to complain about."

For the first time after today's reality check, Jordan allowed herself the thought that they might be okay anyway.

Her resolve lasted a few hours longer. Maybe it was the enormity of the project they'd take on hitting home once more, her gratitude for Ellie's steadfast support, or the sip of wine that had gone straight to her head.

Ellie, who had a sixth sense about these things, walked in on her standing at the sink in their bathroom. She embraced Jordan tightly, and in the privacy of their home, there was no longer a reason for being neutral.

⁂

The big day had arrived, the first time they were going to see Jordan's parents after they'd found out that their plans would be slightly postponed, and the lieutenant had told Ellie to drop the investigation. That was the easier issue, though it still bothered her. Of course, she couldn't have anticipated a new, far-reaching murder case.

Neither of them felt much like celebrating at the moment, but here they were, getting ready for the big opening of her father's bar, covered by local press. Jill Allen would be there, in private, and a colleague of hers would write about the event many in the city had been waiting for.

Jordan caught her look in the mirror.

"My answer's still the same," she said. "It sucks. I'm not going to shatter. We'll try again as soon as possible."

Ellie knew without a doubt that part of her composure was for Ellie's sake, and maybe she had a point. It had been a difficult week, with many questions. But it was true what Jordan had said—they'd try again. There were many options still open for them.

"Of course. We can allow ourselves a night out. That won't change anything."

"Right. Given the fact that my parents will be around, it won't be that wild," Jordan said, making her laugh.

"Not that we've ever done anything that wild...oh wait. Well, we have a home now. I think of all people, Derek has been most excited. He'll be happy."

"Yeah. We all have a lot of memories of this please. Let's make some more."

⟋⟍

Ellie saw through her, like always. Much to her credit, she didn't prod, and they were on their way to celebrate Jack's project, the re-opening of the *Code 7*, now simply *SEVEN*. It wasn't about pretending. Between the two of them, they knew how they felt, and, Jordan reflected, they deserved a break away from it all to have an evening with family and friends.

She noticed the dark van that had stayed fairly close for most of the drive, wondering if she should pay more attention, or if it was possible that the driver's destination was simply the same. Shortly before the last exit, he changed lanes.

"He's not going to the party," Ellie mused. So, she had noticed, too.

"Doesn't look that way."

The bar had been built from the ground after a bomb had gone off, fortunately after they had time to evacuate the place. Many of the people who came to celebrate tonight had no idea about the close calls of that day. Most importantly, Jack and Pauline didn't. Jordan had always made an effort to keep them as much in the dark about the more dangerous aspects of her job as possible—it was enough that Ellie shared them.

"Yeah, I have some mixed emotions about the place, too," Ellie said, making her laugh.

"You're in my head again. I'm fine."

"I know. Just stating the obvious. Wow, there's a crowd here. You better start looking for parking now."

They got out of the car a block from the venue, where people had assembled the unveiling of the sign over the entrance. Built from the ashes. Jordan could relate to that image, and for the first time that day, she felt truly excited.

The cover fell away to reveal the name of the new bar, spelled out in tall letters:

SEVEN.

"Welcome! Make yourself at home!"

Jack was making his way through the crowd shaking hands, until he had reached them, Pauline not far behind. Jordan was relieved they hadn't told them yet.

The *SEVEN*'s opening night was a resounding success. The place filled up right away—the *Code 7* had been popular, but its numbers had been dwindling over the years. Hopefully, the trend would go the other way now. By a sheer miracle, they had found some of their friends and managed to score a table. Waiting for drinks took a little longer than usual.

Jordan caught the surprise on Casey's face when she saw her sipping her beer and shrugged in her direction. *Not this time. Not a subject for tonight.* Casey had understood every bit of the non-verbal communication. She gave a smile and went back to her conversation with Libby.

There were many familiar faces, from their precinct and others. Noah Shriver stood in a corner with a Missing Persons detective, Rogers.

"Excuse me for a moment, I'm just going to say hi," Kate piped up. During her last weeks with the PD, she had worked on a case with Rogers. Derek followed her with his gaze, commenting, "Look, it's your new best friend."

That was for Jordan, and she decided that he definitely felt like he had missed something during his absence.

"That's not what I would call it."

"You got any leads in the Callum murder yet?"

Jordan sighed. "There I thought I had the night off. And no."

"There might be something I could help you with. But don't tell Major Crimes yet."

"Mac?" she guessed, surprised. Derek's trusted CI had been a great help when it came to arresting major drug dealers, but she didn't think he had connections to the kind of crimes they suspected the McDonalds of.

"I'll see what I can do and let you know."

"Great. Thanks."

"No problem. So, how is...everything else?"

"Everything is good, why do you ask?...Oh, I see. You had a conversation with Kate—after she had one with Ellie."

"Sorry," he backtracked quickly. "None of my business—or hers, for that matter."

"Well..." She raised her beer. "That's your answer. Not much happening there either, and to be honest, I didn't want to think about work or babies tonight."

"Understood. But wow, this place is something else. Jack and his friends did a great job. Will be nice to have something in walking distance again."

"Yes, definitely." Jordan appreciated his attempt to direct the conversation into calmer waters again, though his earlier proposition regarding the open murder case intrigued her. She was going to come back to that.

"I see that pool table is free for now...You're up for it?"

"Sure. Whoever wins pays the next round."

Ellie had many things on her mind, trying to chase them best she could as she listened to Kate relate her and Derek's adventures while camping north of the border. She was listening attentively enough to affirm her notion that she and Jordan preferred a firm roof over their heads, and a queen-sized hotel bed whenever possible. But Kate was happy, and near glowing, and Ellie was happy for her.

She also kept an eye on Jordan, part concern, part self-indulgence. Her body language conveyed clearly that she kept winning, which did something to Ellie, though she wondered when the one beer, the exception, had turned into something else. She wasn't going to say anything, not because of one evening. Being the designated driver for the night, Ellie wasn't drinking. She saw Detective Shriver join Jordan and Derek and suppressed a smile. Derek would not be amused. Ellie of all people understood Shriver's ambition. She just thought he was trying too hard and hoped she hadn't come across the same way. Or if she had, that she was doing a good enough job to prove that she was where she belonged. Her musings led her back to George Wilder, and the unsolved new case.

It was hard not to think about work in a room full of cops. That had never bothered her before, but for some reason, tonight, it did. If the wrong man had been arrested sixty years ago, both Stella Brown and George Wilder still hadn't gotten justice, and a murderer might still be alive and free. She couldn't let it rest. Not when the Callum case barely required her with its connections to the McDonald couple that were covered by Major Crimes and other Homicide detectives.

"Yeah, I know, you haven't heard a word of what I said the last ten minutes."

"You saw a real moose in the wild."

"Wow, you're good. What's your mind really on?"

"How long it would take me to get another drink, and if my wife is winning enough to cover a round for all of us. Come on, let's check."

If Noah Shriver solved cases like he played pool, Jordan had decided that he was welcome in Homicide, not that it was up to her as she'd reminded him a few times. Maria Doss had teamed up with Derek. She was good, too, but they were no match for Jordan and Shriver. Jordan knew it would be a good idea to ease up on the drinks, but she enjoyed leaving all responsibility aside for the moment. She had barely given herself enough time to enjoy all the ways her life had improved in the past few years, with Ellie by her side, sharing a home, marriage...perhaps they had a tendency to go for the next best thing a bit too fast. On the other hand, there wasn't so much time...As she had told Derek, she was happy to forget it all for one night. Another round of beers had softened the men's territorial feelings.

They, like Jordan, were flabbergasted when A.D.A. Esposito arrived, late to the party, and greeted Maria with a kiss that left the observer with no doubt as to the nature of their relationship.

"So," Valerie Esposito asked cheekily. "What did I miss?"

Jordan was asking herself the same question, not that it mattered. Whenever she or Ellie weren't the subject matter of gossip, it was a good day in her book—and it looked like Doss and Esposito didn't mind.

⁓

"Oh, that. I completely forgot to tell you," Ellie admitted as they walked to the car. She was trying to figure out how she had trouble keeping up, even with her wife slightly blitzed. She guessed her own heels made them even.

"You knew? Wow. How is that possible?" Jordan undeniably had questions of her own.

Ellie suppressed a sigh. She had gotten used to having to work with one of Jordan's exes, or another, but she didn't like to make them a subject under the best of circumstances.

"Doss was dating Derek for a while, you remember, right? He didn't know either."

"I do remember. Bisexual people exist."

"Yeah, you're right. That just surprised me. Wow."

Ellie suspected that their conversation might not have happened the same way, had Jordan been sober.

"You still won the game, element of surprise aside. Shriver seems like a good player too."

"Yes, we did pretty well—"

She had barely spoken those words when the vehicle sped past them, its tires touching the edge of the sidewalk for a few tense seconds. Ellie nearly lost a shoe when Jordan pulled her into a doorway, but the driver didn't direct the car onto the sidewalk, just turned and sped away.

"And there you thought I was drinking too much tonight," Jordan remarked dryly, though the tight grip she kept on Ellie belied the casual tone.

"I'll never underestimate you. I also have a partial license plate, and I think I know who we are looking at."

Chapter Ten

"You kept those at home?" Jordan asked with only a hint of criticism when Ellie opened the file.

"Not the time. I didn't recognize the car earlier, but I'm sure I've seen that plate before. And here it is. Jamie already had a few DUIs. I'm calling it in. If he didn't mean to hurt anyone, he might soon."

Jordan didn't argue, even though it was obvious to the two of them who this warning was meant for.

Over the phone, Ellie gave the license plate number and model of the car, Jamie's name, and a description of the incident. She was aware that while she sounded fairly calm, her throat tightened at the memory. It was hard to tell at this point what his intentions might have been. Better not to take any chances. She left a message for the officer in charge to let her know once they found him.

Jordan would have loved to spend this time of night curled up next to Ellie in bed—as it was, they found themselves back in their workplace reporting an incident that couldn't be a coincidence. Ellie had been told to let go of the Wilder case, but it seemed that Jamie Ryan didn't believe she had, following her to her car then following them tonight, twice. Subtle wasn't his strong suit—he had to know that they were aware of his record. Unfortunately, they didn't have enough to go on tonight.

Neither of them was in the room with the suspect. They were both watching from the other side of the two-way mirror.

"This is harassment," Ryan claimed. "Yes, I talked to one of your detectives, and she even sat down for a coffee with me. We talked, that's all. My great-aunt is very fragile. There is no reason to drag her into all of this."

In the glass, Jordan could see Ellie roll her eyes.

From what she had told her, Jordan did not consider Ms. Montgomery fragile at all.

"You deny you were following her in her car tonight? And the incident on 12th street?"

"I didn't follow her. That was coincidence."

"Twice in one night?" the officer asked skeptically.

"Okay, not the first time. I recognized the car—I saw the article that the investigation was officially closed, and I thought of asking her about it, but then I saw she was with someone."

"He's lying," Ellie said. "He knows my car, not yours."

"Look, I've been careful since those DUIs, okay? I lost my license for a long time the last time. I learned my lesson. I did not drink or consume anything tonight."

"Then how do you explain steering the car onto the side-walk?"

"I didn't. It just happened...it's a new car, and I think they gave me a lemon. I'll take it to the shop tomorrow."

Ellie made a non-committal sound and went to join Jamie Ryan and the officer in the room.

"Oh, hey, Detective. Why don't you tell them...?"

"That was my wife's car you were following earlier," she said coolly.

Something in his expression changed. Ellie wasn't if it was because she'd caught him in a lie, or because she'd used the word wife.

"I don't give a shit what you do in your private time. Just leave me and Enid alone."

"Or else?"

"You said that. All I wanted was to ask you about the damn article. Why can't you let it rest? Wilder killed that woman, and many people suffered as a consequence, including my great-aunt. She deserves better than to be harassed by some—"

He caught himself in time. "By the cops."

"Why don't you speak freely? I'm interested in your opinion."

"Forget about it. I didn't try to run into you, the car malfunctioned. That's all. Am I free to go? I swear, I won't come near you, and I hope you'll do the same for Enid."

"As you said before, the investigation is closed. Good night, Mr. Ryan"

Ellie left the room, frustrated as she was aware there was nothing they could hold him on. Her grievances with Enid Montgomery, and suspicion that she might have raised Jamie Ryan in the same bigoted way, didn't count.

❦

Detective Shriver wasn't present at the Monday briefing. A.D .A. Esposito had come in and updated them on the McDonald case, while expressing her frustration that they hadn't made any progress regarding the Callum case. The murderer seemed like a ghost—no one has seen anyone with Callum after he went back to his room, and the cameras hadn't yielded anything helpful.

"Maybe someone switched the recordings," Ellie mused, only realizing when all eyes were on her that she didn't mean to say it out loud. That was a little too much like on TV, wasn't it?

"We checked with security," Jordan took her thought seriously enough to give an answer. "They are all clean, and no one else had access to the room."

"What about the cameras?"

"They were working. This guy's freaking invisible."

"Well, maybe not," Derek suggested. "I spoke to Mac. We can see him later tonight."

"You do that. Anything else? I hear there was an incident related to the Wilder case this weekend. Harding?"

"Montgomery's grandnephew. She raised him after his parents died. There wasn't much we could do, but I think he got the message."

"Make sure he did," Carroll said. "I want you to go over the witnesses' statements again. You," he addressed Jordan and Derek next, "head over to Major Crimes and see where they are. And call me with whatever you get from your guy right away."

Everyone was getting to their feet.

"Oh, and Carpenter, tell your dad congrats on his business. Didn't I hear somewhere it was supposed to be named Carpenter's?"

"No sir," Jordan answered with a terse smile while Derek could barely hide his amusement. "That was never the plan."

❧

Even while spending most of the day going over the witnesses' statements from the day Callum was murdered, Ellie made a few moments of time to research Jamie Ryan during her lunch break.

Like her own parents, Jamie's had died in a car accident. Unlike the tragic deaths of Patrick and Meredith Harding, Ellie soon found out that the circumstances of Jamie's parents were a lot more mysterious. The investigation concluded that his father, the driver, had lost control over the vehicle and driven it off the road where it plunged down a steep ravine. What she read made Ellie shudder, and she had to force herself to separate that story from her own. She needed to pay attention. It was a sunny day, no evidence of another car on the road, nothing obviously wrong with the Ryans' car.

Strange, that Jamie, too, claimed to have lost control for a moment.

This case consisted of a number of strange occurrences and coincidences...but she wasn't supposed to work it any longer on the department's time.

With a sigh, Ellie went back to the statements, until one particular name jumped out for her. She'd hold off on calling Jordan and Derek until she had something solid to show them.

Mac was as jumpy as Jordan had ever seen him, and he usually had a reason. The diner where they met wouldn't be her usual choice for dinner either, but a mix of disappointment, hormones, and frustration about the slow pace of this case made her vulnerable to the lure of junk food.

Asked about the McDonalds and their money-laundering scheme, he shook his head. "Hey, they are small fish, in comparison."

"Who are the bigger fish, then? Why wouldn't they give them up in order to save themselves?"

"I don't know that much more."

Jordan sent a questioning look to Derek, who shrugged. Were they wasting their time? Jordan hadn't forgotten that the one time Mac asked to see her alone, she got hit over the head. His information usually panned out, but it could be sketchy at times.

"So, what are we getting out of this other than the pleasure of your company?"

"I'm telling you, dig deeper. Promise them something."

"Like what? They are already stinking rich, and so is their lawyer."

Mac shrugged. "Like I said, small fish. You need to see the bigger picture. I might be able to hook you up with someone who can help with that, but that will cost you."

Derek regarded him closely.

"You on something? You remember the deal we have."

"No, no, I'm not!" Mac insisted. "Just trying to be careful, I swear. Those people don't care about a few bodies in a convenience store, and I sure as hell don't want them to get to me."

"We'll talk to the McDonalds again," Jordan said. "But you need to give us something more."

"Look into their foreign business contacts. Russia."

She suppressed a sigh. That would involve other departments and agencies far beyond cooperation with Major Crimes.

"The banks that gave them money, and who's running them," Mac continued. "What they wanted in return."

"How soon can you hook us up with those more knowledge-able people?"

"Give me a week or two, do your homework."

If there was a jibe in it, Jordan let it slide. Their food had arrived.

⚬

"Everything okay?" Derek asked as they were heading back to the department half an hour later.

Jordan was still trying to determine if the greasy burger agreed with her. It was probably better not to give it too much thought.

"I'm fine, thank you." That might be a bit of an exaggeration. Ellie had been right, she'd been drinking too much this past weekend, and Jamie Ryan's motives were still somewhat shady. Sure, not everything in life had come to her easily, so why would having a baby? Maybe she was running out of patience.

Derek didn't ask for details. Instead, he brought their conversation back to the case.

"Perhaps you could ask your friend at the FBI. Your new friend," he added, but even so, Jordan had assumed he was talking about Agent Torres, not her ex, Dr. Bethany Roberts. Truth be told she wasn't looking forward to involving either of them, but if she had to, she'd probably go with Nina Torres first.

"Could be worth a try," she agreed. "We'll do some research on the McDonalds first, and check with them before Mac gets back to you."

"Sure. We tell Shriver?"

"Not yet..." She shook her head, amused at his reaction. "I thought that whatever it is you two are territorial about, you came to a ceasefire?"

"I haven't made up my mind yet."

"About Shriver or the ceasefire?"

"Both."

"Oh well, suit yourself. I'm going to call Carroll and then check if Ellie's ready to go home."

"Sounds like a plan."

Ellie had a number of printouts spread over her desk. She knew that the credit card number of the business who had canceled the room belonged to an escort service whose name had been all over the news not long ago. That might be the reason they had tried to lay low...She had done an image search on the Internet and after only a few minutes, found what she'd been looking for: A picture of Marius Callum at a fundraiser, with Teresa Hartford, the owner of the escort service. Of course, that was only a seldom talked about part of Hartford's business, but here she was, smiling into the camera with Callum. She searched more about the event and found her suspicion confirmed—the Mc-Donalds were mentioned in a small paragraph. The fundraiser had taken place in the past year.

She would pay Teresa Hartford a visit the next day.

As if on cue, Jordan and Derek arrived.

"Just in time," Ellie said. "You might find this interesting."

Ellie had been nowhere near the car accident, away in college when the cops knocked on her door to bring the horrible news. She had imagined it over and over again, enough for it to become vivid in her nightmares. They had become rare, almost non-existent, replaced by the occasional memory of encounters with serial killers and garden-variety misogynists acting up. Close calls, hers, Jordan's, the friend they lost.

She had spent a lot of time in the past lately. The odd coincidence of what she and Jamie Ryan had in common brought everything bubbling to the surface again, and Ellie woke with the feel of tears warm on her face.

She wasn't the only one awake.

"Hey," Jordan said softly. "You're with me? What was that about?"

Ellie took a shaky breath, as she let herself be embraced. Warm. Safe. Real.

"I sort of understand what got Jamie so messed up."

Jordan's fingertips brushed over her shoulder.

"Yet, you don't have a record a mile long, and you don't try to run people over."

"You have a point. I just meant that I can understand why he's so loyal to Enid despite her bigoted ideas. She took care of him. He was lucky."

Ellie had been too, in a way, she was aware. She had been old enough to be able to live on her own. Jamie Ryan's fate could have a different one if he didn't have Enid.

Jordan's story could have been a different, much worse one, if it wasn't for Jack and Pauline.

"It doesn't excuse the way either of them acts, but it's true."

Perhaps Jordan had the same thoughts, and that made it easier for Ellie to voice her concern.

"We need to make sure all papers are in orders. That our child is taken care of whatever happens."

"And we will." Jordan moved her hand to Ellie's cheek, leaning in for a kiss. "She or he will never have to worry."

"One more thing on the list." Ellie sighed. "Sorry for waking you. You've had a long day too."

"Yes, but fairly productive, like yours. Good call on Hartford. You mind if I come with you tomorrow?"

"If Carroll doesn't, no, but why? I don't think it's going to be any dangerous."

"That wasn't my point," Jordan whispered. "I like watching you call their bluff."

Somehow, the atmosphere had changed from post-nightmare solace into something entirely else. Ellie didn't mind.

"That's good to know. In that case, feel free to come along."

Her next dreams would be sweet.

Chapter Eleven

C arroll didn't have any objections, and so they left Derek with his research on the McDonalds' foreign business contacts and drove to Teresa Hartford's office.

Jordan had left a message with Nina Torres to get back to her as soon as possible.

Hartford, whose name was connected to hair salons and spas scattered all over the state, had them wait. Jordan had expected nothing less, and she hadn't made an appointment for a reason. Meanwhile, she and Ellie sat in the posh waiting area, declining the coffee that Hartford's secretary offered them.

"Clearly, it pays off to be a Madam, huh?"

There was no way the twenty-something secretary could have heard Jordan's commentary, but she glared into her direction anyway.

"Right, perhaps I should have taken that coffee."

"I'm sorry. I kept you up."

"It was for a good reason."

They shared a smile, and Ellie almost questioned the wisdom of taking Jordan to this interview, after spending a good part of the night cuddling and planning the future, for them and the baby that would be part of their family. She and Jordan had been working together for a few years now, starting when Ellie was still in uniform. Usually, she didn't get distracted but today felt different.

They had made it through some difficult times. Early on, they sometimes had tiptoed around each other, afraid to cross lines. These days, it was so much easier. They could talk about everything.

"Detectives?" The secretary put her phone on her desk. "Ms. Hartford will see you now."

"Thank you!" Ellie jumped to her feet, Jordan following her into the spacious office. Spacious was a vast understatement, actually. Whatever it was that generated most of Hartford's income, it was lucrative.

"Detectives Carpenter and Harding." Teresa Hartford had clearly paid attention to the information the secretary had given her about her visitors. The woman in her early fifties shook their hands with a polite smile. "Homicide." She wasn't smiling anymore, though her tone stayed cordial. "I understand that there have been some misunderstandings with the police about parts of my business before, but I can't imagine I could help you with a murder investigation."

"This won't be long," Ellie said. "You might have heard about the death at the Capitol Inn?"

"How could I not? It was all over the news."

"The room next to the victim's had been rented by your company."

"Is that so? I'd have to check that to be sure. I don't do that kind of scheduling, as you can imagine."

Ellie could. "I was hoping you could look into why the reservation was canceled a day before the incident, and if someone might have been in contact with a Mr. Callum."

Hartford regarded her with calculation in her gaze.

"Detective...Harding, it is, right? You have a warrant? I'm not running a prostitution ring, as I've been accused of before, but this is still sensitive information."

"We were hoping you could do us a favor," Jordan, who had remained silent so far, said. "Just so we know there's no connection between your business, and a murder case."

"I guess if I swear to you there isn't, my word isn't good enough? Give me a moment. I'll check that for you."

"We appreciate it," Ellie said.

Hartford sat behind her desk and typed something on her computer keyboard while Jordan seemed to take an interest in the artwork decorating the wall. Ellie had a hard time keeping herself from tapping her feet.

"And here it is. A Mr. Meyers booked one of our employees for dinner and conversation but then changed his mind. That's why we canceled the room as well."

"Why did you book a hotel room when the relationship between the client and your employee is supposed to be strictly platonic?" Ellie asked.

"For backup," Hartford said, as if that was obvious. "Some of my employees work from out of town. It also has happened before that a client tried to change the rules of the contact, and I don't want any of my girls kicked out on the street."

"I see...Can we have that information?"

Teresa Hartford hesitated.

"It would be very helpful to us, and we can take it from there," Jordan suggested. "We probably wouldn't have to bother you again."

Hartford hit the print button.

"Okay, but be careful with that information." She handed the pages to Ellie, then, on second thought, picked up a business card. "Actually, you weren't bothering me at all," she said as she held out the card to Jordan.

"Remember, we don't do anything illegal here...and if that's of any interest to you, we serve women, too."

∾∾

"I hope that's of no interest to you," Ellie said when they were back in the car, amused and still a little amazed at how they'd gotten that information.

Jordan chuckled. "God, no."

"Good. I almost had trouble telling the difference, the way you turned on the charm with her."

"I didn't."

"Oh yes."

"Well, we got what we wanted, right?" Jordan reached for her phone and checked her messages. "Okay, Derek says to meet him over at Major Crimes." She picked up the pages that Hartford had given them and started skimming over them.

Ellie, keeping her eyes on the road, asked, "How is that going? With Shriver?"

"Fine, now that he and Derek have set the ground rules." She shrugged. "I guess. Nothing from Nina yet. I suppose it's not that urgent on their side."

"Let's find out."

∾∾

To Jordan's surprise, Nina Torres was waiting for her in the conference room with Derek, Shriver, and a man she didn't know but appeared to be FBI.

"Hey, good to see you," she said with a smile. "Looks like you stepped into a hornet's nest—again. Congratulations."

Jordan wasn't too sure about the metaphor, but she supposed they'd get some details soon. "Wow, you are fast."

"Not that fast," Torres admitted. "We were in the area. I don't have to tell you that we have to be careful when it comes to specifics, as I need to protect the identity of some of my colleagues."

"Because of the McDonalds' foreign dealings?"

"I do like the way you think. Now let's all sit down and put together what we have. I'm fine with giving you the McDonalds if you have enough to prosecute them here, but anything beyond that is ours."

"They got a lot of money from international banks in recent years," Derek said. "Looks like Russian banks were on that list. We're not entirely sure yet what they offered in return."

"They said Callum wanted money from them," Jordan recalled. "How much did he know?"

Nina exchanged a look with her colleague.

"What?"

"Let's just say we have an interest in solving this murder as quickly as possible. We are currently doing our own investigation, and that covers some of those foreign connections."

"Callum was undercover?"

All eyes were on Ellie within a split-second.

"Asset." Nina said. "That's not leaving this room, am I clear?"

"This case has been dragging the whole time," Noah Shriver remarked. "And you didn't think it was important to let us know earlier?"

"There's more on the line than I can talk about at this time. Callum was supposed to test the McDonalds. He swore they weren't on to him, but it doesn't look that way now, does it?"

Jordan was still trying to get all this new information straight in her head. The couple with ties to foreign banks. Callum and Hartford. Borrowing money from various sources wasn't necessarily a crime, but it was the sums that raised red flags.

"If they are behind this, they were damn clever executing it," she said out loud. "Nothing on the cameras, no hint that they might have been manipulated."

"What about the escort?" Ellie held up the sheets. "We just came from Hartford. This wasn't the first time Callum booked with the agency. There might be a connection."

"If it's about big money, there's a good chance it's connected to the McDonalds somehow. Could be those came from investors for a lavishing resort that was never built. Drugs, human trafficking. You might want to take a closer look at that agency too."

"I can do that," Ellie offered.

"Good. We are setting up here at Major Crimes for the moment," Nina declared. "Anything else?"

"I'm waiting to hear from my informant," Derek said. "He promised to put us in touch with someone who can give us more on the McDonalds and the money trail."

Nina regarded him pensively.

"The people we're looking at are well-connected, and in some cases, pretty much out of reach, so this would be gold. You trust that guy?"

Jordan winced, reminded of the one occasion Mac's information hadn't been good, leaving her with a grueling headache.

"Yes."

"All right then. Let's find enough to put those the McDonalds away and not tip off anyone else in the process."

It sounded easy in theory.

Once more, Jordan found herself in the car with Ellie. Mac hadn't called yet, and Derek had promised to let her know the moment he did. Meanwhile they were on the way to the escort that Callum had frequented.

Jordan's cell phone rang, and she picked it up, on the other end the person she had least expected: Her former colleague Cliff Waters.

"Hey," she said, unsure what to expect. As long as she'd known him, she'd rarely received good news from the man. He didn't waste any time.

"I'm not sure what the hell you told him, but my dad asked to speak to you again."

That was not something Jordan had expected out of the brief and surprisingly pleasant conversation with Waters senior.

"Really?"

"Says he's been thinking about the case some more. Look, I wouldn't call you if he didn't keep pestering me with it. I want you to wrap this up the next time, okay?"

Jordan suppressed a sigh—not that she expected him to change his behavior, ever.

"If your dad wants to talk, I can make time on the weekend."

She was aware of Ellie's quick, curious sideways glance.

"Same rules. You keep Harding away from me and my family. She's done enough damage."

"And fuck you." She had ended the call before saying those words, making Ellie chuckle.

"What was that?"

"Just Waters being himself...but it turns out his dad has more to say."

"On the case I was told to let go," Ellie reminded her.

"Yeah. I don't know if I didn't have the heart to tell him no—the dad, that is—or if I didn't say anything because I know this is pissing off Waters. As far as I'm concerned, he got off too easily."

"Yeah, he did. Well, I'm sure Carroll doesn't mind if we do it on the weekend."

"You're right."

Jordan had every intention of taking Ellie this time.

"How long have you been seeing Mr. Callum?"

Rose's apartment was a one-bedroom, but the layout, furnishing and décor, not to mention city center location, revealed to the casual observer that she had a considerable source of income.

If she could afford to live here, how much money did Hartford make? Ellie wondered. And did she have an illegal side business behind the legal escort service? She'd been investigated before. What had they missed about all those curious connections? One thing was for sure—lots of money was exchanging hands.

"On and off over the last two years." She was wringing her hands in her lap. "I can't believe he's dead! He was so nice, never questioning the boundaries."

"Your last app—date was canceled," Ellie said, unsure what to name it. "Did anyone tell you why?"

"No," she said quickly. "They don't tell me a reason. I get the message, I go home."

Something about that struck Ellie as odd. She exchanged a look with Jordan, certain she had caught it too.

The hotel room had been canceled the day before.

"You were at the hotel on the day? You didn't get the message earlier?"

"No, that's not what I meant. I got a message from the agency saying that he couldn't make it. I never went there."

Rose was a terrible liar.

Jordan, who had been standing so far, sat on the couch across from Rose who shot her a nervous glance.

"What do you want? I was nowhere near the place. I didn't kill him. I told you, I liked him!"

"I believe you," Jordan said softly. "At least, the part where you say you liked him. Don't you want the people who are responsible for his death, to pay?"

"That's your job, right? I know nothing about it."

"Then what are you afraid of? Is Ms. Hartford or anyone else threatening you?"

This time, she held Jordan's gaze.

"No. Ms. Hartford has been great. Actually, I don't have to talk to you any longer, do I? I told you everything I know."

"Okay. If you can think of anything else, let us know."

Chapter Twelve

B y the weekend, Mac had not yet made contact. They hadn't heard from Rose either, and everyone seemed to be more on edge every day. With the McDonalds' court proceedings approaching, they were still following leads on their foreign investors, trying not to step on anyone's toes in the meantime.

Jordan had made another appointment, though the big question was very much in the background at the moment. At least Jack and Pauline had good things to report about their first week of the *SEVEN*, and Jordan and Ellie were going to see them for dinner after meeting with Waters senior.

"I messed this one up," Ellie said with a sigh when they were on their way.

"How so? You gave it as much time as humanly possible. It's not your fault that there was nothing to find."

"But that's the point, isn't it? I brought up some painful memories for a lot of people, myself included..." Jordan remembered the nightmare. "...and others got their hopes up for nothing. When everyone said there was nothing to see, I should have believed them, not waste everyone's time."

"You don't really believe that, do you?"

"I believe that people who hurt others should pay for it. If they're old, or sick, that doesn't relieve them of their responsibility. But maybe there was really nothing to see there."

"A lot about it was really strange," Jordan admitted. She didn't like it either, but Ellie would likely have to live with the uncertainty. "I have to say, I'm a little curious as to what Waters wants to tell us. After that, we'll try to lay it to rest. I'm sure Doreen is grateful that you tried."

"Yeah. I hope so. Okay, let's give this a try."

They met with Joseph Waters in the common room. Surprisingly, Cliff Waters had opted not to join them, either bored with the subject of conversation or not eager to see Jordan again.

A few weeks ago, Ellie would have been a lot more excited about the progress, but it was true what she'd told Jordan. She was frustrated and worried about her apparent lack of instinct when it came to the Wilder case. So many loose ends. Enid Montgomery. Jamie Ryan. Too many sleepless nights had showed her what happened when she was trying to meddle with events past and out of her control. She had to look to her future, with Jordan, and the child they were going to have.

"So nice to see you again, Detective Carpenter!" Waters got to his feet and shook her hand. "And this is...?"

"Detective Harding." Ellie stretched out her hand before Jordan could answer. "Thank you for seeing us."

"It's my pleasure. Cliff doesn't really want to do a lot of shop talk, and what else is there to do?" he said with a laugh. Even after what Jordan had told her about the first meeting, Ellie was surprised. In this case, the apple seemed to have fallen far from the tree.

"Sure. Cliff said there was something you'd like to talk about," Jordan reminded him.

"Oh yes. I haven't thought about this in many years, and maybe it wasn't important...but there were rumors about Stella and another girl. At the time, we only thought that added to Wilder's guilt, that he was jealous, but after we last talked, I remembered...Enid, she seemed to be very taken with Stella. It's still possible that George misinterpreted the signs."

Ellie was both excited and dismayed. Was this detail important after all? But if it was, did it mean they had a cold-blooded lesbian killer on their hands, or had George murdered Stella because he thought she was involved with Enid? Either way, it didn't make much sense.

Or maybe it did. Had Enid's projection and self-loathing led her to kill Stella?

"I saw Enid Montgomery," Ellie told him. "Her home...It's like traveling back in time. She's obviously clinging to the past, but I'm not sure if this is about George, or Stella, or both. In any case, she blew up at me when I suggested she might have had feelings for Stella."

"An odd lady for sure," he agreed. "Lately, I'm wondering if odd enough to take an axe to someone's skull."

"That would be hard to prove though," Jordan summed up their situation. "Did you know her grandnephew?"

"I heard that she took him in after his parents died in a car accident, that's all. I don't know if this detail is important, but I thought you should know, to have a picture as complete as possible."

"Thank you for that. We appreciate it," Ellie said.

"What the hell are you doing here?" Even at a neighboring table, occupants flinched at Cliff Waters' outburst. "Screw you, Carpenter, I told you not to bring her here."

"Cliff, enough!"

"We were just leaving," Ellie said. "Thank you so much, Mr. Waters." They shook hands again, and they left, not before Jordan had a chance to glare at their former colleague. For the sake of the older Mr. Waters, both of them wanted to end the conversation as soon as possible.

It wasn't new or surprising to Ellie that Cliff Waters hated her, for being much younger, with a promising career, and for speaking up for his victim. She wasn't sorry for either of it.

"That was pleasant."

Jordan watched Ellie for any signs of distress. She seemed nothing but frustrated about the encounter.

"He has issues, nothing new there. I feel sorry for the dad. He seems like a decent guy."

"Yeah. Does this change anything for you?"

"I don't know," Ellie admitted. "I had the same idea, and obviously Enid didn't take well to it. Jamie freaked out over the fact that I went to see her again—they are both troubled, but maybe not reason enough to keep going."

To Jordan, she didn't sound convinced.

"What? He said it himself, it might be nothing. I think he likes to talk to other people sometime, especially cops, even better if they're not his jerk of a son."

Despite herself, Jordan had to laugh at Ellie's apt description. She was going to let it go for now, for the sake of a relaxed family dinner. Despite all the warnings she had given, Jordan understood why Ellie was so intrigued with this case. Everyone always seemed to come back to Enid Montgomery, a good friend to Wilder, a caring family member to Jamie Ryan who had ended up with lots of problems nonetheless—though they probably couldn't blame that on Enid. A nice older lady. The next moment, a raging homophobe.

It wasn't quite the transformation that Jordan had seen in other criminals—the smooth polite businessman inviting her for a drink after the deal was sealed, becoming the monster of her nightmares...but it was something.

Not that they had a lot of time to keep investigating a sixty-year-old murder with the multiple connections in the Callum murder and the McDonalds' crime history.

She was tired. It was the weekend. It would have been so easy to have that one glass of wine. One couldn't be too harmful to their prospects, could it? Jordan declined nonetheless. If everything went as planned the next time, she wouldn't be drinking for a long time to come. If it didn't—well, there would be enough time and reason to drink.

Jack, of course, had been busy with all things *SEVEN* in the past months, but between main course and coffee, Pauline took her aside.

"I'm not quite sure how to approach this," she admitted.

"You're not opening another bar, are you?" Jordan quipped.

"No, silly." Pauline shook her head. "You haven't had a glass in weeks, and Ellie either goes along, or is undecided. "If you're trying out something that I don't need to be nosy about, that's fine. I just want to know that you're okay."

Jordan wondered how to tell her the truth without getting her hopes up too high, too soon, not sure she was ready for this conversation. Remembering she'd already had it with Kathryn made her feel guilty. Apparently, she had hesitated for too long.

"You're scaring me a little..."

"Oh no, there's nothing to be scared about. We...Ellie and I...are trying. We want to have a baby."

It still felt a bit odd saying it out loud. "We didn't want to say anything before, and frankly, there's nothing much to say yet, but yeah, that's what it's about."

"That is amazing. I'm happy for you." Pauline hugged her.

Might as well get it all out. "It didn't quite work the first time, but we'll try again. In fact, I have another appointment, and...I talked to Kathryn. I'm sorry. I had to, in order to make sure there won't be any bad surprises."

"I understand."

Those weren't just words, Jordan knew. Over the years, Pauline had come to understand when and why Jordan would come to her...or what subjects she preferred to keep at bay.

"I don't want to get ahead of myself, but you know we'll help any way we can, right? Have you talked to anyone at work?"

"Thank you, we really appreciate that, and I'm still figuring things out."

Her cell phone vibrated on the counter next to her. Predictable. Her being somewhat relieved was also predictable, especially when the caller turned out to be Derek.

"Hey, what are you doing at the moment?"

"Waiting for you to text me an address, I assume, since you call me on a weekend. Mac called back?"

"He did. You're up for it?"

"Sure. Should Ellie come too?"

"Not this time," he said. "This person's a bit jumpy, Mac says, so it's just me and you."

"All right then. See you in a bit."

Pauline's affectionate smile spoke volumes. "I suppose that means you won't be staying for dessert," she said.

"Sorry about that. It's urgent. Let me go talk to Ellie for a moment?"

A few minutes later, she said goodbye to Ellie after quickly updating her. "Oh, and I might have let something slip about our plans, so that will likely be the subject of conversation over dessert. Sorry." A quick kiss, and she was on her way.

Jordan met Derek where he had parked in a side street, in an area where detached houses and duplexes gave way to non-descript apartment buildings, all looking like the same grey blocks in the dark. They walked from there, and he updated her on what Mac had revealed over the phone.

"They have about twenty minutes, but he claims it will be worth it, says they can tell us more than he ever could."

"They?"

"Figure of speech."

"All right. I hope this is good enough to drag me away from Pauline's blueberry pie."

"Come on. You enjoy it too much, and you know it. Nothing wrong with that, by the way. We might have the big break by Monday."

"Yes, that would be great." Not only because she'd love to tie up the Callum case neatly before moving on to other, bigger things in her life. There would always be a case, and she'd have to live with at least some loose ends in the coming months. Derek was right, though, she enjoyed this, and she suspected he did, too.

Their lives had taken amazing turns lately, but there was something exhilarating about dropping everything for the chance to outsmart some bad guys.

She hoped this information would be good enough to wipe the smug smiles off the McDonalds' faces—and their lawyer's.

Mac waited for them in the shadow of a hedge, hands in the pockets of his hoodie. He didn't look anything out of the ordinary, though he was older than most of the people around here they'd seen sporting the same style.

Jordan thought of Darla, her friend and former informant. She had managed to help her get off the streets, but not before an incident that left Darla barely alive. She was doing well now, working and taking care of her young child. In the near future, it was more likely that Jordan would ask her for advice.

"Come on, hurry up. You guys are already not subtle."

He led them around the towering building and across the alley towards an abandoned barber shop. Part of the logo was still visible in the window, and there were patches on the wall where, Jordan assumed, mirrors had been. A single chair sat in the middle of the room.

"This is all interesting," she said. "Now where's the mystery guest?"

"Come with me."

They went to a backroom, and from there, down a few stairs behind another door.

"Mac, you remember what we talked about," Derek warned.

"Man, don't I always?"

"Good evening, Detectives."

Jordan felt her jaw drop at the sound of a familiar voice.

Chapter Thirteen

To Ellie's relief, Jack and Pauline didn't pursue the subject for too long—as Jordan kept reminding all of them, there wasn't much to talk about yet. They had a long list of things to check, but for most of them, there would be enough time once they were actually expecting—like turning the guest room into a nursery.

It occurred to Ellie that they would have to talk to Ariel, the teenager they'd rescued from a misogynistic, murdering cult. They had been all set to start adoption proceedings before a blood relative, Ariel's aunt, showed up and took Ariel in. That guestroom was supposed to be Ariel's. Ellie made a mental note to call soon, as they hadn't heard from her in a while.

No message from Jordan yet. It was getting late.

"I guess I'll have to call a cab," she said. "We have an early start tomorrow."

"Have another piece of pie, and Jack can drive you after," Pauline suggested.

It was hard to say no to that, though Ellie couldn't entirely get rid of the strange feeling that had gripped her. Perhaps it still had to do with Waters' outburst, or the way it reminded her of Montgomery losing all politeness in an instant. People could change in a split-second. She hoped that Mac was still true to his word.

She would have loved to see a message telling her everything was okay.

No such luck.

Teresa Hartford looked very different from the wealthy self-assured businesswoman they had met the other day. In her jeans and old leather jacket she blended in more than Jordan and Derek did in this neighborhood.

"Well, now you know my secret. I want the McDonalds to go away, and the people who are keeping them afloat."

"You know who killed Callum?"

"I know that they gave the go-ahead, same with the frame job on Driscoll, because they got too close. Callum got made."

Jordan came to the conclusions quickly. "It's not the first time you work with the police, I assume. Is it true what you told us the other day, that all of your business is legal, or did someone look the other way?"

Hartford almost looked offended. "Does it matter? I'm giving you names. You'll solve a murder and have something to give to your friends at the FBI."

"The agent said something about human trafficking," Jordan remembered.

"Obviously, I'm not involved in any of that, but I hear things from some of the women who come work for me. The McDonalds and their friends want to keep their lenders entertained, and sometimes they take measures to make sure they don't change their minds. But that's only a part of it. They launder money through modeling agencies, and sometimes, real estate. It's a bloody mess."

"Sounds like it. Was Rose one of the women who told you those stories?"

"You leave her alone, okay? She's doing well, and she's not involved in anything illegal, I swear. That has to be enough."

She could tell from Derek's expression that he would have preferred to refocus the discussion, but she had to make sure.

"Is she in danger?"

Teresa Hartford gave a wry laugh. "Honey, aren't we all? Look, somebody was in that room with Callum. It wasn't Rose, but she did go to the hotel that day. The message didn't come in until an hour before the meeting. She waited at the bar. He showed up as planned, they talked, but he said he didn't have time, so she went home."

"He was trying to protect her?"

"Hell if I know. I don't think he expected to end up with a bullet in his chest though."

She couldn't let this go now. "Rose was quite nervous when we talked to her. Did she tell you anything else—about someone she saw, maybe?"

"No. Like I said. She had a bit of a crush on Callum, but she doesn't know anything."

Jordan didn't mention that this kind assurance might not be enough for the people who had killed Callum.

"All right, about those names?"

"I have a bad feeling," Jordan said when they were back in the car. "Let's swing by Rose's apartment."

"Now? We'll have a ton of work to do tomorrow morning, and if I'm not mistaken, you left your wife at your parents'?"

"All of this is true, but...Humor me. This story about the cancellation, who did it and why, and Rose seeing Callum shortly before he died...It's making me queasy."

"Maybe you had too much pie?" One look from her convinced Derek to change lanes and take the exit to the area where Rose lived. "Fine. Let's just make it an all-nighter."

⁂

They earned some suspicious looks from the couple in the elevator. Jordan didn't care. Everyone involved had some big secrets, the McDonalds, Driscoll, Callum and Teresa Hartford. It wasn't too big a stretch that Rose might have stumbled over something that put her in danger—she was too close to some of these people. If Teresa's information panned out, they might be able to arrest a lot of people come tomorrow. Some of them might want to cover their tracks.

In front of #506, she knocked on the door. "Rose? It's Detective Carpenter. Please open the door."

There was no answer. The sinking feeling in the pit of her stomach only grew stronger. Rose had been nervous about something already. The inconsistencies regarding the canceled appointment couldn't be a coincidence.

"Rose? I know it's late, but this is important. I promise we won't be long."

A man hurried past them, keys in hand. He turned around. "Can I help you?"

Jordan showed him her badge. "Please, go to your apartment."

"I'm sure there's someone we could call," Derek said after the tenant had followed her request. "You don't have to...All right, too late, I guess," he acknowledged after she'd kicked in the door.

Taking a deep breath, Jordan stepped into the apartment, making her way to the living room where she and Ellie had sat not long ago. It was eerily silent, almost impossible that someone wouldn't wake up from the noise, unless they were on heavy medication, or...If she turned out to be completely wrong, she'd take responsibility, but she usually didn't kick in doors on a hunch that didn't have any foundation.

The smear of blood on the hardwood floor only confirmed her suspicion. Hand on her gun, she went to the closest door, a bathroom that was empty. In the master bedroom, a lamp was turned over, more blood on the king-size bed. Walking around it, Jordan nearly stumbled over Rose's lifeless form. She dropped to her knees, searching for a pulse, relieved when she found one. Derek was already calling an ambulance.

Looking up, she saw the bedroom window open, the blinds half torn down—probably this was where the intruder had come in and escaped from. If they were lucky, he wasn't far.

"Hang in there," she urged the unconscious woman.

Tomorrow, the McDonalds' bail could be revoked. It was about time.

⌒⊙⌒

Ellie sighed to herself when she listened to Jordan's voicemail. Jordan had suggested that one of them should get some sleep, since the next day would be predictably hectic after a successful meeting with Mac. Worst case scenario, Ellie could bring her a change of clothes in the morning.

Ellie didn't feel much like sleeping, and she thought she could make herself useful. Pauline had supplied her with half of the pie. If a night shift helped with having a head start the next morning, her colleagues might appreciate it. First of all, though, she went to meet Jordan and Derek at the hospital where Rose was still fighting for her life.

She had been shot once, the injury leading to grave blood loss.

"They don't know if she's going to make it," Jordan said with a sigh.

"If she does, it's because of you," Derek reminded her. Jordan shrugged, obviously not satisfied with the odds.

"It's curious though. If it was a professional hit, and in this context, we assume it was, I'm surprised they didn't make sure she was dead." Ellie winced, but she thought she did have a point. "Were they interrupted?"

"It's possible," Jordan said. "Why aren't you at home?"

"I thought you could use the help. Do you need anyone to stay here?"

"Doc says he's going to call as soon as Rose is able to talk—we'll know in a few hours, best case scenario—or if anything else changes. No. There's a ton of paperwork in the future. I guess we can get started on that."

"Time to wake Esposito?" Derek suggested.

"Soon," Jordan said. "What is it?" she asked a moment later.

Ellie had been distracted by the man she'd seen turning the corner. She might have been mistaken, but...

"Wait a second," she said, leaving the two of them standing. They had assumed that Jamie Ryan would keep his promise now that the investigation was closed...An odd coincidence that he should show up here after they'd visited the older Detective Waters again. Remembering the scene that Cliff had made, Ellie shook her head. But how would Jamie know?

She decided not to confront him, just follow and see what he was up to. From a distance, she could see the man entering a room. When Ellie saw who the patient was, she knew that she hadn't been mistaken. That, however, made it unlikely that Jamie had followed her. Just another strange coincidence.

She had to shift her focus once again.

"What was that?" Derek asked when she joined him and Jordan again.

"Looks like Enid Montgomery was hospitalized," Ellie said. "I thought I saw Jamie...But obviously he's not here because of us. Sorry about that, we have other things to do."

She was curious, though, about why Enid was here. That was a question for another day.

When they arrived at the station, Ellie was surprised at how busy the place was already. Agent Torres was in with Lieutenant Carroll, and Detective Shriver stood close to Jordan's desk, looking unsure whether he should sit or not.

Eventually, Carroll stepped out. "Ladies, Gentlemen, I hope you enjoyed your weekend while it lasted. We have to move fast, so there's little chance any of you will get home before tomorrow evening. If you need to stock up on coffee or anything else, you better do it now. Harding, what is that?"

"Blueberry pie."

"Sounds good to me. Let's get started."

⁂

Esposito joined their meeting less than an hour later, delighted with the wealth of evidence Hartford had given them.

"This is going to make waves," she said when she and Jordan were alone for a moment. "I can't wait to bring this to my boss. With all that money floating around them, the McDonalds are definitely a flight risk. And considering what's in their future, they might be a little more eager to cooperate."

Jordan felt less optimistic at the moment. For once, she was tired—she hadn't yet gotten used to cutting down on the caffeine. There was no news on Rose's condition.

"The informant isn't going to testify though," she said. "There's a lot at risk for them. That's why we met in some dingy basement."

"There are a lot of names on this list." Valerie wasn't having it. "Have a little faith. Rose might be able to describe Callum's murderer, and we already have a couple of likely suspects here."

"I hope this works out. This is such a mess."

"You're in a hurry," Valerie remarked. "More than the usual."

Jordan shrugged. "I don't like chaos."

"Hm."

"What's that supposed to mean?"

"Oh, nothing. Don't worry. This is good. We'll have to work out something for Rose afterwards."

"Yeah." Jordan wasn't really sure why she did it, but maybe it was because Valerie never had a problem asking nosy questions about her private life. "So, you and Maria? Congrats."

"Thanks. And I could say the same to you, taking it to the next level?"

Case in point.

"I guess I deserved that. Well, it's not as easy as it looks, but yeah, now's the time."

"Good luck with that anyway," Valerie said warmly. "We've all been through some crap. Bring on the good times."

"That's right. Unless you were talking about us...?"

"Honey, aside from the fact that you had a girlfriend, it wasn't so bad. I regret nothing." Her expression grew serious. "Don't tell anyone, but Maria went through a pretty nasty break-up. Let's say if I ever meet the guy, I'd be tempted to abuse the powers of my office."

This was complete and disconcerting news to Jordan, and she wasn't sure why Valerie had chosen to share it.

"If there's anything I can do to help..."

"No, thanks. I just needed a little venting. All right, now that we have that covered, let's go back to work."

"I like the way you work here," Noah Shriver said.

She wanted her body to cooperate, Jordan reminded herself, create the best possible circumstances for a pregnancy. She still wanted to grab his coffee and drink the whole cup.

"Did you talk to Lieutenant Carroll?"

"Not yet. Things are a little too busy at the moment."

"No kidding." She suppressed a yawn. "Well, you keep trying. We've had a few slow weeks around here, but as you can see, it's not like that now."

Her cell phone rang, and Jordan excused herself. "Detective Carpenter? This is Dr. Hunt. Ms. Myles is awake."

"Thanks for letting me know. I'll be right there." Ending the call she said to Shriver, "You want to come, or would you prefer to go knocking on doors with Henderson, checking on those names the informant gave us?"

She knew it was a rhetorical question.

At least she wouldn't have to deal with the delicious smell of real coffee any longer.

Officers Sam Potts and Casey Lyons had been assigned to guard Rose's room. Dr. Hunt appeared right before they were about to go in.

"There are some ground rules, Detectives," he warned. "Ms. Myles has been through a lot. A few minutes, not more. For everything else, you need to come back."

Jordan wasn't going to argue with him, and Shriver followed her lead.

"I hear that...you found me."

She had to lean closer to understand what the young woman was saying.

"I'm not sure if that's...a good thing. They're going to come after me again...and Teresa." Jordan cast a quick look at Shriver, wondering if he had heard all of it, and what he was making of it. There was a reason why they couldn't reveal where most of those names had come from.

"You'll be safe, I promise."

"Others have promised before."

Had both Teresa and Rose worked with the authorities?

"We've been told that you talked to Mr. Callum the night at the murder, and he left you at the bar. Did you see who he was meeting with?"

Rose nodded, the fear stark in her wide eyes.

"Was it the same man that broke into your apartment?"

A tear formed in the corner of her eye, rolling down her cheek.

"You knew that already. No one...can ever get to them."

"You're talking about the McDonalds?"

"No. Their handlers."

"Detectives. I need to ask you to leave. My patient needs her rest."

"She also needs protection from dangers outside of this room, and we can provide that best if we have all the information we need," Jordan told me. "Just one minute." She leaned in again.

"Rose, honey, I'm sorry, but we need their names."

Hunt looked irritated, Shriver pensive. She couldn't use either of them in the room at the moment. "Could you leave us alone? I swear, Doc, we'll be out of your hair in a few seconds."

"One minute," he said. "Or I'm calling security."

"You too, Noah. Please." He might not be interested in what Derek had been insinuating, but it wasn't a secret that Shriver liked her. At the moment, Jordan wasn't above using that.

"I'm not sure if—"

"Come on. You don't want him to call security on us?"

When she was alone with Rose, she said, "We are protecting Teresa as well. She gave us some names, connections, but if you could confirm them, it would be a great help. We could arrest some of them as soon as today."

"Okay then." Rose's voice had the broken tone of a person who had no hope, and nothing left to lose, but she confirmed every single name on the list, some American, some Russian.

Jordan vowed she'd pull every string possible to prove her wrong. She assumed that some of those men were likely no longer in the country, out of reach. They could still be named in an indictment. It was important they'd look at all of their contacts, in case one of them still presented a threat to Rose.

"You get better now," she said, touching the woman's hand gently. "That's all you need to worry about. We'll take care of the rest."

Chapter Fourteen

At the end of a long, but satisfying day, Jordan rang the doorbell at the McDonalds' mansion. Nina Torres as well as a couple of uniforms accompanied her and Shriver. After almost a minute, the door opened—an instant later, Mrs. McDonald nearly slammed it in their faces.

"You have no right to be here. I'll file a complaint—"

"Feel free." Jordan held up the paperwork put together based on the day's arrests, statements and evidence that corroborated the couple's involvement in various crimes—including framing Driscoll, and the hit on Rose. "First of all, you'll have to come with us."

"What? You can't do this. Our lawyer—"

"I advise you to call him when we're at the station. Where's your husband, Mrs. McDonald?"

"He's not here," she said, her denial quick and hardly credible.

Jordan let Shriver deal with her and pushed past the woman, Nina on her heels as they hurried to the upper level of the house, where bedrooms and McDonald's office were located.

The sound of a gunshot nearly stopped her cold in her track. As much as she didn't want to go past that door, she knew she had to.

"Mr. McDonald?"

There was no answer. Hand on her gun, bracing herself for the possibilities, Jordan pushed the door open. McDonald sat at his desk, staring at the gun in his hand.

"Put it down," she said.

He laid the weapon on top of a folder. McDonald was unharmed, but the painting on the wall to the left side had seen better days.

"You made the right choice," Jordan said, not even trying to keep the relief out of her voice. This could have been so much messier...triggering. She didn't have to go there.

Startling her, McDonald laughed as Nina read him his rights and put the cuffs on him.

"Save it," he said. "You have no idea who you're dealing with. You just should have shot me. That would have been easier on me and you."

"We have a lot to talk about now," Nina told him. To Jordan and Shriver she said, "Thanks, Detectives. I think my people will take it from here."

❦

"That was...abrupt," Shriver remarked when they were back at the station, wrapping up for the day.

"Get used to it if you're interested in more of those interdepartmental gigs in the future." She scanned the room, but Ellie was nowhere to be seen. No message from her either. Jordan couldn't imagine that she'd feel like going out after the workday they'd just had.

"At least the McDonalds will go back to prison unless they give up some big-time connections, and no one got shot. That's some good news. Can I buy you a drink?"

"Are there any bad news?" Jordan asked, stalling on his question.

"It's all relative. I did have some time today to talk to your lieutenant. He said that there's no opening at the moment, but when there is, he'll consider my request."

"I'm sorry, but we already had a replacement for Waters. He just stayed on a few months longer."

Too long, she thought. She respected Lieutenant Carroll, but perhaps Waters had been given a little too much leeway, especially in recent years.

"Yeah, I guess all I can do for now is wait. What about that drink?"

"Oh, hey, there you are." Ellie had saved her. "I know you were probably planning on going home, I was too, but I promised Kate to meet at the *SEVEN* for an hour or so...We could have dinner?"

"Sure." To Noah Shriver she said, "I think my wife will pay for my drink tonight," hoping to lay those particular implications to rest.

"Another time, then," he answered. "I hope this is not the last time that we worked together."

⌘

"I was right, admit it," Derek claimed, earning a shrug from Jordan in reaction. Perhaps he was right after all, but Shriver wouldn't be working with Homicide so soon. Besides, he had likely gotten the message by now. They had other concerns. She would have liked to have a beer with the delicious sandwiches and fries served at the *SEVEN*, but she couldn't break that discipline now.

Along with their hopes and dreams for a family, there was a serious amount of money on the line every time this didn't work out. Also, if it did work out. The new appointment was coming up, and the idea filled her with both excitement and dread—because there was a chance it would turn out exactly the same way, and then what? They wouldn't give up on a family, but she might have to give up on the idea of giving birth to their child.

"If that gets you off my case, sure," she said. "He's trying to make friends. Carroll's not going to have him before the end of the year."

"You used the term wife," Ellie reminded them. "There aren't many ways to misinterpret that."

"Stop it. No one's misinterpreting anything. Anyone wants to get me another ginger ale?"

Ellie, of course, supported her new alcohol-free habits she'd only broken for the *SEVEN*'s opening—but she couldn't ask the same thing of Derek, Kate, and their other friends.

"You were saying?" Derek chuckled at the sight of Noah Shriver who had just walked in, waving to them.

Jordan sighed.

Ellie knew that this appointment was a whole lot more stressful for Jordan than it was for her, though she could barely hide her excitement. While she hadn't been happy that Carroll had taken her off the Wilder case, they had made great progress with the McDonalds and their connections, and they were back on track regarding the family planning. She'd keep the words of Waters senior in mind.

All was well, wasn't it?

In the waiting room with them were a man and a woman in their thirties, and another woman who was obviously close to her due date. Ellie had a hard time tearing her gaze away. It was coming true for them, too. It had to.

"You're staring," Jordan whispered, making her blush.

"I guess I'm a little impatient, that's all."

Jordan laughed. "That's a new one."

"Forget what I said. It's all perfect."

The woman got up and walked past them to a rack of flyers, giving Ellie a smile that made her even more flustered. She was relieved when the doctor's assistant opened the door to the waiting area.

"Ms. Carpenter?"

Jordan's hand felt cold in hers, and Ellie was reminded that she'd have to keep her own, bubbling over emotions in check for a bit.

❧

Jordan and Derek had gone to see a witness last thing in the evening, while Ellie was catching up on paperwork. For once, the plan was to have a quiet evening at home, with dinner and a little TV. Predictably, when Ellie closed the last file, her cell phone rang.

"Detective Harding? You said to call if we could think of anything."

It took her a few seconds to recognize the voice of Emily Brown, Stella Brown's niece.

"Ms. Brown, hi. What can I do for you?"

"Stephen and I had hoped you could come over. You see, we had a lot of conversations since your last visit. I swear we never had any doubts that George Wilder was the murderer. We wanted him to pay. Aunt Stella's death...it destroyed our mother."

"I understand," Ellie said, not yet sure where the conversation was going.

"Still, if there was an innocent man in prison, I think she would want to know that some idea of justice was served in the end, and of course, so would Stella. You remember that the police had some letters and a diary of Stella's?"

Ellie sat up straight in her chair. If those had held any hints regarding the murder, they would be in the evidence box? At the very least, she would have seen them mentioned somewhere in the reports? Cliff's anger be damned, she might have to see his father again.

"Where are those now?"

"The police gave them back after they looked at them, said there was nothing important in there. I think Riley and Patterson were their names."

So that had happened before Waters senior joined the investigation. Did he know about the letters and the diary?

"We have them here. I don't know, maybe you agree with your colleagues, but I think there are some things you should look at. Just to be on the safe side."

"I'll be with you in a bit," Ellie promised. "What made you look at them now?"

"It's not like we read them many times. It was a painful reminder, but now...I don't know. Maybe some of it looks different with the distance. Please, I need you to tell me I'm not crazy."

"There's a number of people who had doubts," Ellie admitted. "Thank you for calling. I'll be right over."

She called Jordan from the car and left a message.

Jordan had mentioned the threats made by McDonald, about unnamed people coming after them, though she hadn't given them much weight. They were mostly the FBI's concern now. There was Cliff Waters' unpredictable temper. Officer Chris Atwood, Waters' friend, had suggested Ellie might find herself without backup at a critical moment, for turning Waters in. He'd been reprimanded.

All in all, those events might be the reason why she felt like someone was following her, let alone the fact that Jamie Ryan had made it his mission to make sure no one contacted Enid again.

Perhaps she was just tired. Ryan wouldn't be so careless to follow her once again in the same car, and besides, he couldn't know about Emily's call.

She and her brother seemed to have waited by the door, because Emily opened it before Ellie had a chance to ring the doorbell.

"Thank you so much for coming," she said. "We all want to let this go once and for all."

"It's been a long time," Ellie agreed. She followed them into the living room, where a box sat on the coffee table.

"You can take these," Stephen said, "but there are a few passages we wanted you to look at. "Mom always told us what the cops had said to her. We didn't want to prod and hurt her, but it looks like Stella was madly in love with Wilder. And she was afraid of Enid Montgomery."

"Did she say why?" Ellie could feel her heart beat faster. All hints seemed to point at Enid, yet she'd never been considered a suspect?

Stephen took the leather-bound book and opened it to a page he had marked with a sticky note. "It's not entirely clear, but I assume that since the three of them always hung out together, that E. is her. Stella was confused by her behavior."

E. can be peculiar, Ellie read. *She doesn't like it when I spend time with George, gets so jealous. When I try to talk to her, she gets angry, as if I'm the one accusing her of something.*

"I'll take these, thank you," Ellie said. "I promise I'll get them back to you as soon as possible."

She hurried home, where Jordan had started making dinner, and sat the box on the kitchen table.

"I can't wait to get to these, but it smells delicious. What are we having?"

"Chicken pot pie." Jordan laughed at Ellie's surprised expression. "Not home-made. I picked it up on the way home. I'm afraid I'm not quite there yet."

"Oh, no, this perfect. I'm actually starving. Stella Brown's niece and nephew gave me some documents."

"That's a surprise. I thought they were opposed to re-opening the case?"

"They were, but this seems interesting." Ellie sighed. "In fact, I guess, it's circumstantial, more that we can't prove. But there's something there...Enid being jealous and aggressive. And homophobic."

"Projection?" Jordan suggested as she lifted the pie out of the oven.

"If I were to guess, yes. Problem is that guessing is all I can do after all this time. Also, the investigators didn't think these..." She gestured to the box, "...were important. Someone dropped the ball, but one of them is dead, and the other was very reluctant to talk to me. That was before Cliff's dad came on board. They didn't mention those letters, or the diary, anywhere."

"It is all very curious," Jordan agreed. "How about we'll have dinner, and we'll go over them later?"

"Thank you. At this point, I find it hard to figure out what to believe."

In spite of the heavy subject matter surrounding these documents, there was something compelling about this testimony of Stella Brown's life. The young woman didn't mince words, when communicating with her boyfriend, or talking about day-to-day occurrences. Some of the communications were surprisingly graphic. Yet, she had this puzzling, slightly dysfunctional relationship with Enid, who wasn't a popular girl, but smart. Towards the end of the read, it seemed like she was seeking some distance, up to the moment where she voiced her frustration with Enid's lack of respect for her boundaries. *I said George will take me, and she shows me the new dress she bought. She doesn't understand. George never says anything, but I think he wishes she'd give us some time alone, that I'm indulging her.*

"He had no reason to be angry at Stella. In fact...I don't think George was angry at anyone. Enid obviously was. I wish I could get a warrant for her house."

"To find what?" Jordan yawned. "Stella wasn't murdered there. They had the weapon. It might be an interesting trip down memory lane, but no judge will sign up on that."

"Not yet."

Chapter Fifteen

After breakfast the next day, they parted ways, Ellie going to work, Jordan stopping at the hospital to check on Rose as promised. There was still an officer in front of her door, but she looked a lot better than the last time they had seen her.

When she was about to leave, someone called after her, "Jordan, hi!"

She turned around to see Becca Crane heading her way. Jordan didn't know she was working here. She must have started her job recently. Jordan had done a thorough background check on the woman once it was clear that Ariel was going to live with her, instead of moving into Jordan and Ellie's guest room—future nursery. Fingers crossed.

"Good morning. I was just seeing a witness..."

"Yes, I heard you found her. She was lucky. Look, would you have a moment to join me for a coffee?"

Checking her watch, Jordan said, "I have a few minutes. No coffee though." At Becca's surprised look, she said, "Trying to cut down on the caffeine."

"I didn't think that was ever possible in your job, or mine, but good luck."

"Thank you. Is there anything in particular you wanted to talk about? Ariel is okay?"

"Ariel is great." Becca opened the door to a break room. "Actually, it's about her. You're sure you don't want the coffee?"

Jordan wasn't sure at all, but she had made a commitment. "Yes. Thanks."

"All right. Like I said, Ariel is doing fine. I was just wondering if she could stay over the weekend after next. Mariah will be on a field trip with her class, and we are out of town for work."

"Of course, that's no problem." They had promised Ariel that she was always welcome. Jordan had some questions though. Her silence hadn't gone unnoticed with Becca.

"Yes, she has made a couple of friends in school, but we want to be careful. Right now, Ariel is focused on us, and a few people she trusts, including you and Ellie. She doesn't like staying over with friends, but I didn't want to leave her alone either."

"She's been through hell."

"Yes, I'm aware of that. And she's been making great strides with the therapist as well—it's just that area we're still working on. If you and Ellie are okay with having her for the weekend..."

"Absolutely. I'll let Ellie know, but she'll say the same thing."

"Great. Thank you so much. I'll have Ariel call you for the details soon."

"You haven't talked to her yet?" Jordan couldn't help it. While she had set aside her suspicions for Ariel's sake, she still worried about the young girl.

"I will. I just wanted to check in with you first. I have to get back to work now." She picked up her coffee. "By the way...when are you due?"

For a moment, Jordan was speechless.

Becca laughed. "I'll admit, I was guessing, but the only time I gave up coffee was when I was pregnant with Mariah. Half the time, I wanted to snatch it from other people, and half the time the smell made me sick."

"Oh...I'm not. Not yet that is. We're trying."

"That's great. I wish you all the best. Just be careful when breaking the news to Ariel, in case there is news...She's a bit sensitive where that subject is concerned."

"I can imagine. You don't have to worry."

As Jordan walked back to her car, she thought back to the cult Ariel had grown up in, of which most members were now either serving prison sentences or had lost custody of their children. Multiple "marriages," sometimes with underage girls, had been the norm. It came close to a miracle that she had escaped that fate, and even so, girls had to work and take care of the younger children.

Ariel was smart and perceptive though, and Jordan had no doubt she would understand the difference.

Not yet.

But I want this so much.

⁕

Ellie had diligently worked without breaks, so she could sneak away for an unannounced visit to Waters senior. She caught him at dinner. His face lit up when he saw her.

"Detective Harding. Good to see you again."

"I'm sorry to disturb you. I just have one quick question."

"Nonsense, sit down and if you like, have dinner with me. God knows I pay enough for this place."

"I think this is for family members?" Ellie had to admit that the buffet looked amazing.

"Well, you don't see any family members here, do you? Don't worry. I told Cliff I could meet with whoever I wanted to. I have no idea what got him so upset...but I get the feeling he regrets retiring."

Not wanting to wade into that conversation, Ellie said, "I think you're right. They're not going to throw me out over a plate of food, are they?"

He winked, giving her a smile.

So, Waters had still not told his father that he hadn't retired as planned. He'd been fired weeks before the date for sexually assaulting a young officer. It wasn't up to her to clear that up.

She sat back down with her plate.

"Were you ever aware of Stella Brown's diary, or the letters she wrote to Wilder?"

He gave that some thought. The silence stretched on for so long that Ellie feared he might have forgotten, but then he spoke.

"I think Riley mentioned them once. He said there wasn't anything important in them."

"I found no record whatsoever. Stella's niece gave them to me, and they are at the very least adding to what you told me the other day. That scene...there was a lot of anger and hate in that act. But Wilder wasn't angry or jealous. From these writings, it looks like Enid was."

"You might be on to something there. What's the next step?"

"I'm not sure. My lieutenant told me to let it go, and we just wrapped up a big case...I think I should talk to Enid again, and Jamie Ryan."

"Be careful," he advised. "Someone's skull got split open, and if Wilder wasn't the one who did it..."

"I understand."

Ellie wasn't going to take any chances, not with everything in her life as perfect as it was.

She decided to make a quick stop at Enid's. The older woman seemed neither surprised nor fazed to find Ellie on her doorstep. Enid Montgomery leaned heavily on her cane, though Ellie noticed that she had opened the door within seconds after the first ring.

"It's the young lady with a penchant for the past."

"Good evening, Ms. Montgomery. I saw Jamie at the hospital the other day, and I wanted to see how you were."

For that, she earned a dubious look.

"Do you really care? You gave our family a lot of sorrow."

"I'm sorry about that. It was a misunderstanding that we cleared up with Jamie."

"Did you now?" Enid sighed. "You want to come in? You have any more questions about George...and Stella?" She coughed.

Ellie had many questions, though she was still debating with herself how confrontational this conversation was supposed to be.

"I've been talking to a lot of people. Many said that you and Stella were close. I'm sorry for all the pain this must have caused you, then, and in recent weeks."

"Come on in, Detective," Enid said. "You would have found out either way."

A plate with cookies sat on the coffee table. "I made tea if you'd like...?"

"No, thank you. I had dinner earlier."

"You're running around talking to us old folks about things we barely remember...I hope they pay you well at least. See...George was angry at Stella. Very angry, and for a reason. Of course I'd never thought he would kill her over it, but...She had those unnatural tendencies, and he found out about it."

Ellie braced herself. Yes, she wished she could change people like that, no matter their age, but a confrontation wouldn't help her case.

"She had a relationship with another woman?"

"I told her it was going to end badly. She would have no more friends, though I tried so hard to bring her back on the right path. George found out...and that was it. I sensed something the night we all went to that party. It wasn't just murder. It was a lesson for all of us."

At this point, Ellie wasn't taking anything she said at face value, though the emotions, the anger, seemed rather real. She'd witnessed the same behavior in Jamie—nurture over nature, in this case.

"Killing someone with an axe was a lesson?"

"The axe was maybe exaggerated, but we still put people on death row as a deterrent, don't we?"

"Wait." Her words made Ellie's stomach churn. "You're not equating what he did to Stella with the death penalty?"

"Why not? Sure, it's harsh, but in other places, they do it."

"There was no mystery girl, was there? You wanted Stella all to yourself, but she was in love with George. Not just in love. Maybe she even told you some of those graphic details she put into her diary, and the letters she wrote to him."

"Sweetheart, you have no idea what you're talking about."

"Oh, I think I do. You were in love with her, but you loathed yourself for it, and besides, Stella wasn't interested in anything but friendship. I don't think George even knew about any of it. He was the perfect scapegoat."

"That is very impolite of you."

"A woman died!"

"Yes, and I told you everything I know about it. You're defending her so much, I'm starting to wonder. Now leave my house."

"Some of the original investigators are still around. They remember things too."

"Are you accusing me of anything, dear?" Enid asked. When Ellie hesitated, she smiled. "I didn't think so. Good night."

❦

There was some calm before the storm. Ellie joined Jordan and Derek at the *SEVEN* for a non-alcoholic nightcap. Jordan told her about her conversation with Becca Crane, and Ellie mentioned her after-work activities in passing. They made it an early night, though sleep wasn't on the agenda for the most part of it.

They had a working breakfast with A.D.A. Esposito and Detective Maria Doss, when Ellie's phone rang, and an enraged lieutenant spoke before she could say hello.

"Harding, what the hell is wrong with you? At what point didn't I make myself clear when I told you to let it go?"

She was speechless for a few seconds.

"Lieutenant Carroll...I did a couple of follow-up interviews on my own time..." And besides, Jamie Ryan did follow us. We had to let Ryan go, but that doesn't mean..."

"I'm not talking about Ryan," he said curtly. "Where are you? I need to see you in my office now."

Jordan who had only caught Ellie's part of the call, understood nonetheless that this was serious.

"I'm coming with you," she offered.

"No, that's okay. If you can catch a ride..."

"No problem," Valerie Esposito said.

Ellie left the café before Jordan changed her mind. She was alarmed by the tone of Lieutenant Carroll's voice, one he had never before used with her, but she was certain she could handle this situation by herself.

She was still fairly certain when she knocked on the door of Carroll's office, and walked in to find him with an unfamiliar man and...Cliff Waters? Now she had an idea why her colleagues had given her strange looks when she came in.

"Sir?"

Waters shook his head with a condescending grin.

"Detective Harding, this is Mr. Kellen, an attorney for Mrs. Enid Montgomery. They think it's necessary to file a restraining order...against you. I was hoping that we'd be able to clear this up once and for all."

Ellie realized immediately that she had very little chance to set the record straight, so to speak, with Waters and the attorney present. Lieutenant Carroll didn't seem inclined to ask questions in private first.

"I'm sorry," she said. "There was new evidence, and I know I should have informed you first before I followed those leads."

"There is no evidence against my client," the attorney said, sounding irritated. "She's a senior citizen who'd prefer not to be harassed by the police."

"Speaking of which." Waters, no surprise here, looked like he was enjoying the situation. "I told you to leave my father alone." His expression darkened. "Seriously, Harding, what is wrong with you? He had a mild heart attack yesterday."

"What? Is he all right?"

"He'll survive, not that it's any of your business."

"As a matter of fact, I'm representing Mr. Waters as well in this matter," Kellen said. "Lieutenant Carroll, I advise you to educate your detective on the gravity of her situation. We'll hold off on the restraining order for now, but if she comes near Mrs. Montgomery or Mr. Waters again, her career will be over."

"I'm sorry—" she tried.

"Thank you, Counselor." Carroll ignored her. "I assure you there won't be any more problems."

"Good, then we're on the same page." He and Carroll shook hands, and then Kellen turned to leave. Cliff Waters gave her an amused glance before he said, "Nice seeing you, Lieutenant." He left the office as well.

A few seconds passed by without any word. Ellie still stood in the same spot, stunned by what she'd heard.

"Sit down, Harding. Let's talk."

"I think Enid Montgomery murdered Stella Brown. She was attracted to her, but she hated both herself and Stella for that attraction. In addition to that, Stella had no intention of breaking up with Wilder. Enid killed her and framed him."

"That is an elaborate theory."

"She had means and motive. The investigators ignored some of the evidence, for whatever reason. I am sure that she did it."

"But you can't prove it, and she isn't going to confess."

"So, we let it go? If she was a war criminal, we wouldn't say, oh, she's old, we can't prove it anyway, so we let it slide?"

"You're out of line," he said. "You heard what her attorney had to say, and believe me, I wasn't happy to see Cliff Waters back in here. I wanted you in my unit, because you showed a lot of promise, and your record, so far, spoke for itself. Don't throw it all away."

"What do you suggest I do?" she asked, resigned.

"Don't speak to Waters or Montgomery. Look at everything you have, take an officer to help you with that if you need it."

At her surprised look, he said, "I don't appreciate people threatening me or my detectives, but you crossed the line. There need to be consequences."

Her head was spinning.

"You're not suspending me?"

"Not yet. You keep a low profile for a while. I'm warning you, if you can't do that, it's still on the table."

"Understood, sir. Thank you."

Chapter Sixteen

At home, she tried to support Jordan's new habit for decaf, but Jordan wasn't anywhere around, and Ellie needed to think. In the break room, she ran into Officers Potts and Atwood. Potts, one of Waters' victims, and Atwood, who had supported him until the end, seemed like an odd couple. Potts had the patience of a saint, or perhaps Atwood was starting to behave less like a jerk. In any case, Ellie had something to say to both of them.

"Hey. Sam, if I could borrow you today?"

Atwood shrugged, as if he was the one who had the final say on this. Ellie had already made a call to Sergeant Bristol, her own former supervisor.

She had to swallow her pride for what she was going to do next.

"Chris, wait a second. I heard about Cliff's dad. Please let him know that whatever differences we have, I hope he recovers soon. I would tell him myself, but—"

"Yeah, Cliff doesn't want you anywhere near his old man. Maybe you badgering him even triggered the episode."

"Well, if you visit him, please tell him I wish him well. Thank you. Sam?"

The younger officer didn't bother to hide her relief.

"Jesus, I don't envy you," Ellie exclaimed when they were out of earshot. "Sorry. It's been a day already."

"Well, mine is looking up," Sam said. "What do you need me for?"

"I'm not sure you'll be thanking me at the end of the day. Lots of paper to go over."

Something was nagging at the back of her mind, coming back to her even after the turbulent morning.

Montgomery's lawyer teaming up with Cliff Waters, accusing her...what had Enid said about talking to "old folks"? Was it a general figure of speech, or, had she for some reasons been aware that Ellie had approached Waters senior? And he had a heart attack the same night?

Something was off. Was it paranoid to think there was something strange about the sudden heart attack of a man who had seemed in good health?

This time, she didn't take any risk but laid out her theory to the lieutenant right away. He agreed that she might have a point. More of a politician than she was, he involved both Waters and Officer Atwood.

Ellie couldn't care less about the credit if this actually led to something, preferably back to Montgomery and Ryan.

She could have walked to the *SEVEN* from the station, or texted Jordan to meet her at home...but half an hour later, Ellie found herself still driving around, wondering what had possessed her. She had dealt with her grief over her parents, her anger at Natalie.

There was so much in her future she was looking forward to—no, she always came back to the same thing. Her inability to let go of the case wasn't for personal reasons, or anything in her own past she was projecting. Montgomery's blatant homophobia bothered her, but there was more to it. She was convinced that the woman had murdered her friend.

Ryan might or might not know about it, but in any case, he was protecting her, and Waters' interference didn't help. Of course, to him it was personal, and he wouldn't waste a chance to get back at Ellie. She parked the car and took out her cell phone. It wasn't that late, but already dark as the weather had been instable and rainy all day after a brief sunny period. When she and Jordan had been to breakfast with Valerie and Maria. That seemed like forever ago.

She needed a good night's sleep.

She needed evidence for what she knew had happened.

The sound of a gunshot, and then two more, sounding closer, quickly jolted her out of her musings. Ellie called for backup.

⁂

"What the hell is your problem?" Jordan wasted no time finding Officer Atwood in the squad room and getting up into his personal space. His back was against the wall, and that wasn't a metaphor.

Chris Atwood flinched, but given the audience, he pulled himself together quickly.

Jordan didn't care about his feelings or the audience. She had spent the past few minutes in perpetual disbelief and anger at what she'd learned. IA would launch an investigation, but she wasn't sure that would be enough for her.

"You're asking *me*? You're in my face!"

"You bet I am. Are you out of your damn mind? When you hear 'shots fired,' and an officer requesting backup, you don't fucking turn around and get dinner. You were a couple of blocks away!"

Somehow, this wasn't turning out like she imagined, because words weren't by far enough. She wanted to punch him. She might have done it, if it wasn't for Sergeant Bristol thundering, "Detective Carpenter, Officer Atwood, my office! Now!"

Atwood had the audacity to smirk at her before he obliged. Jordan followed him.

"Look, boss, it's not true what they're accusing me of—"

"One at a time," Bristol interrupted. "Carpenter, what is this about?"

Jordan took a deep breath. Bristol had always liked Ellie. He wouldn't let this slide. Then again, no one should. Ellie could have gotten hurt.

Or worse.

"I know that Atwood got a second chance when he first made threats to Detective Harding..."

Atwood snorted.

"But this is too much. He was right there when she requested backup, yet it took another officer fifteen minutes to show up! He threatened to do exactly that, if you remember."

"I remember this very well. Atwood, what were you doing out there?"

The younger officer shrugged. "My job? My radio wasn't working. I couldn't hear anything, so I was about to drive back to the station."

"Bullshit! All the squad cars coming your way didn't tip you off?" Jordan asked sarcastically. "Sergeant, he put the life of another officer at risk. I want to see this addressed. Libby Marshall will want to talk to you as well. She was the one who answered the call when it turned out that Atwood was ignoring it."

"I wasn't—"

"Oh, save it."

"Where is Detective Harding?"

"In interrogation. A suspect in the shooting was arrested."

160

So much had happened in less than two hours, she reflected. Jordan would have loved to take Ellie home, but she had a statement to give, and Jamie Ryan was picked up not much later. Ellie had assured her she was fine to continue, if alarmed that it had taken so long for backup to arrive.

After a conversation with Libby and checking in with the dispatch officer, Jordan had soon found out the reason why.

"All right. Is Lieutenant Carroll still in the house?"

"I think so."

"Good. Officer Atwood, you might want to get in contact with your union rep. I'm suspending you, pending further investigation, but I'm warning you. This doesn't look good."

Jordan wished she could feel some satisfaction at this development. As it was, she still wanted to punch Atwood, and she suspected the sentiment wouldn't go away for some time to come.

"Detective Carpenter, you don't need to be here for this conversation."

"Wait a minute," Atwood protested as she got to her feet. "You can't suspend me for her crazy accusations!"

"Unfortunately, you did make those threats before. I was hoping you weren't serious, but this doesn't look like it. As I said, get in touch with the union rep."

"You bet I'm going to fight this. First Detective Waters, now this, it's all political bullshit!"

He was out of the office before Jordan, nearly slamming the door in her face.

The adrenaline had long worn off, leaving Ellie with a mix of fatigue and an alarm she couldn't quite turn off. She wasn't hurt, she was safe here in the interrogation room with Jamie

Ryan, yet she couldn't shake the feeling that the worst wasn't over yet.

Being shot at would do that to a person. But why?

She wanted answers, and she had convinced colleagues and her supervisor that she was the best person to get them. For some reason, she had gotten under Ryan's skin—his, and that of a few other people, obviously. She didn't want to make any guesses, not when so much depended on her to keep focus...but it had been odd, very odd, and frightening, to wait this long for backup.

Nevertheless, she had seen the van speeding away, and caught enough of the license plate to know it was Jamie's.

"You have it in it for me and my family," he claimed. "Why can't you just leave it be?"

"Because your vehicle was at the scene of a crime. The gun that my colleagues found in your house matched the bullets that went into a street sign right where I was parked. If you have any explanation for that..."

"I didn't drive it," he claimed, and Ellie barely refrained herself from rolling her eyes.

"It was still warm, right there in your driveway."

"I didn't drive it," Ryan repeated. "Someone's out to get me. I wouldn't be surprised if it was one of your colleagues."

"You should be careful, making accusations like that. What about the gun?"

"It was planted. The police do it all the time, don't they?"

"No, they don't. I see you don't want to help yourself."

She got up half-hoping he wouldn't react. Ellie was more than ready to call it a day.

"You keep coming after me. I won't say a word until I can speak to my lawyer."

"Would that be a Mr. Kellen?" she asked sharply.

"So what? I didn't do anything. We're going to prove it. I want to call him now."

"Suit yourself."

———

"Nerves of steel," Derek commented as he joined Jordan in the observation area.

"Yeah. She's pretty good."

Her partner wasn't fooled by the quip. Jordan had no problem admitting that for a few moments, she'd been terrified. The anger that came after that was just as taxing. She ran a hand over her face.

"What a day. This is bad enough, but Atwood? I always knew he was a jerk. I didn't know he was that much of a dangerous one."

Derek nodded. "Yeah. Makes you wonder if someone should have done something sooner."

"Like with Waters? Sure. We all screwed up." She shuddered, thinking how much those omissions could have cost them. "I don't get it. Waters was obviously covering stuff up, but Atwood? Comes from a family of cops. He was pissed at Ellie, but risking her getting killed?" Her stomach did a flip-flop at the thought.

"That is fucked up, even for him," Derek agreed. "I guess we'll find out more during the week."

"Let's hope so. Right now, we should wrap this up. Chances are the lawyer won't be ready for anything before tomorrow."

Her cell phone rang, and Jordan saw that Ariel was the caller.

"If Ellie comes out before I get back, could you tell her to wait for me?"

"Sure," Derek said, turning back to the glass.

When Jordan walked out, she saw Carroll come in. After her encounter with Atwood, she was glad to be on the phone. Jordan was sure she'd hear about it, if not later today, then tomorrow.

"Ariel, hi. How are you?"

"I'm good. You met Becca this week?"

"Yes, I ran into her at the hospital."

"Did you talk about...the business trip?" Ariel's hesitation came across clearly.

"We did. If you'd like to spend that weekend at our place, we'd love to have you over. Just let me know when to...hold on a second." The commotion on the other side of the door told her something unexpected was happening.

"Ariel? I'll have to call you back."

❧

"Just one more thing," Ellie said. If she couldn't make any headway now, she would at least give him something to think about overnight. "Did Enid talk to you about the new evidence that emerged in the Wilder case?"

She hadn't expected him to answer, let alone answer like that. Jamie Ryan lost it, jumped over the table with surprising speed and flexibility, and wrapped his hands around her throat. Ellie hadn't let her guard down around him for a minute, but the ferocity of his actions still startled her. She'd barely blinked before Derek and Lieutenant Carroll were in the room, prying Ryan off of her. Jordan also arrived, helping her to her feet while a couple of uniformed officers steered a resisting Ryan out of the room.

It wasn't a good day when it was already the second time Jordan looked at her with this expression of utter fear.

"I'm okay," she said, coughing immediately. Ellie felt herself starting to shake. "Damn it," she croaked.

"I want you to get your wife to the hospital, now." That was for Jordan. Judging from the tone of his voice, Carroll wasn't having a good day either

"Oh, come on. Sir. I just want to go home."

"That's an order."

Jordan managed a halfway convincing smile. "You heard what he said. After that, we'll go home."

It didn't get much better from there. Waiting in the ER didn't improve her mood, but it wasn't like Ellie had a choice. When a doctor finally saw them, his concern was obvious.

"You don't have to call the police. I'm the police. This happened earlier at work."

"Okay. Officer..."

"Detective. Harding," she corrected him.

He carefully examined the affected area, wincing. "All right. It looks like you'll be fine, but it will be painful for a bit."

"No kidding."

"I'd like to have a scan done anyway, to be on the safe side."

"Is that really necessary?"

"Thank you, Doctor." Jordan's tone didn't leave any room for negotiation, and so Ellie resigned to another wait. Fortunately, it only took minutes, and the doctor confirmed that his initial diagnosis held up.

"Looks good, but if you have trouble breathing, go to the ER right away, you hear me?"

"Loud and clear," Ellie mumbled.

They bought takeout on the way home, and when they arrived, Ellie went straight to the liquor cabinet to make herself a gin and tonic.

"I'm sorry," she said. "I know I promised...but."

"Extraordinary circumstances," Jordan said, brushing a hand over her back. "I understand."

"Yeah. I don't completely understand all of it yet, and it bugs me. On the other hand, I don't want to think at all right now." She emptied almost half of the glass in one sip, taking a deep breath as the alcohol hit.

"We'll talk tomorrow. I just have to call Ariel quickly, and we can make it an early night."

"That would be great."

Jordan pulled her close, and they stayed like that for a moment long enough to assure themselves that this was far from the worst that could have happened.

⟡

Jordan kept her promise. After dinner, a hot bath, massage and some pain pills, Ellie fell into a surprisingly deep sleep, not waking up until the first few rays of sun stole into their bedroom.

Next to her, the bed was empty. Ellie made a quick beeline for the bathroom where she grimaced at her reflection showing the colorful bruises around her neck. She went to the kitchen where coffee was brewing.

"I made you the real kind," Jordan said.

"Decaf is real."

"Don't I know it."

"...but thank you," Ellie continued. "I'll have to check in...I'm not sure how much time we have until Jamie gets his lawyer."

Jordan took a sip from her own mug, her expression darkening.

"He made Kellen's job a lot more difficult now. They had better play by the rules. Are you sure you're up to it?"

Ellie shrugged. "I guess so. I have to be. He's unraveling, which could help the case. I'm not sure what exactly happened yesterday."

"How so?"

Jordan sat across from her.

"I'm glad I don't have to deal with Atwood for the moment. He's...I don't even have words for that. Ryan, there was something bubbling under the surface the whole time, I'm not even that surprised. But why would he shoot at the street sign when I was right there?"

Jordan looked like she was quite uncomfortable addressing this question.

"Maybe he didn't want to hurt you," she said, then winced. "Not like that, anyway."

"Yeah, but it's still odd. He reacts. Whenever Enid tells him something, he goes off the rails, he thinks she's in danger from us somehow, and he feels like he has to rectify that. He doesn't really consider or care much about the consequences."

"Yeah, well, shooting a street sign isn't much of a rational action either...though I'm glad he took aim at that."

"The gun is registered in his name?"

"As far as I know."

In her mind, Ellie went over the events of the past few days, wondering where she could have overlooked something...and what.

"You don't think this could have anything to do with the McDonalds and their contacts?"

Jordan shook her head. "They're the FBI's problem now. Nina will take care of it, but as we assumed, some of those people aren't in the country any longer, and they have eyes on the others. You said it yourself, Ryan is not the most stable person. He's extremely loyal to Enid, and when he felt like you were getting too close...well, we got proof of his instability."

"You're probably right."

Ellie yawned and reached for her cup again.

"Let's go wrap this up, and...thank you for last night."

Jordan had known, once more, exactly what she needed. Time to get to work. Unbidden, an image of Enid Montgomery sprang to her mind, a woman to whom family mattered a great deal, who had jumped in so her niece's son wouldn't have to be with foster parents. It seemed at odds with her bigoted views, or maybe to her, it wasn't.

In any case, Ellie assumed they hadn't met for the last time.

Chapter Seventeen

llie had been right: Enid Montgomery and her lawyer, Mr.
Kellen, were already waiting for her at the station.

"This is unbelievable," he complained. "There's no reason for making us wait, other than stalling tactics."

"Well, Detective Harding is here now, and we can get started," A.D.A. Esposito stated. "Your client attacked her yesterday, and also, he couldn't reach you until early this morning. We're hardly the ones holding things up."

He seethed but didn't say anything.

Ellie realized that Enid was calmly studying her...and Jordan, who had kept close.

"I'll see you later," Jordan said.

"Sure."

After Jordan had left the room, they all took seats around the big table in the conference room. Ellie had chosen not to cover up her bruises—she saw no reason to cut Ryan any slack at this point. The man in question avoided her gaze, nervously tapping his foot on the floor. Kellen whispered something to him, curtly, and he stopped for a few seconds only to start over again.

"We're dealing with a serious situation here. You followed Detective Harding last night, fired shots close to her vehicle."

Ellie half expected Jamie Ryan to protest, or do something more drastic at Esposito's summary, but he still wouldn't look up. Enid's gaze was stormy. She, too, remained silent.

"When the detective questioned you later, you attacked and choked her. We're on the same page so far?"

"I'm sorry," he said, finally meeting Ellie's gaze. "I overreacted. It won't happen again, I swear."

"No, it won't," Esposito agree, "because we're going to charge you with assault."

"I told you I was sorry..." His voice rose until Kellen laid a hand on his back.

"There was a report of another incident. You were questioned, you apologized, and yet, yesterday happened."

"You said that you weren't driving the van, and that someone planted the gun," Ellie reminded him. "Do you stand by that remark?"

"I was afraid you could trick me into something," he said. "Like you tricked my great-aunt. You were obsessed with proving her guilt and mine."

"What are you saying?" Esposito asked. "The vehicle and gun are yours, no?"

"They are. I'm sorry. I don't know what I was thinking. Enid took care of me all this time. I don't know what I'd do without her."

"Mr. Kellen, a word?"

After he and Esposito spent a few moments whispering in the corner, Kellen said, "Mrs. Montgomery, I'll have to ask you to wait outside for a few minutes."

Ryan sat up straighter, alarmed. "You can say everything in front of her."

"This is necessary. I'm sorry," Kellen insisted.

"I'll be fine," Enid said. Well aware that everyone was watching her, she got up excruciatingly slowly, leaving the room leaning on her cane every step. Ellie wondered if she had gotten that much worse since she first met her.

When the door had closed behind Enid, Esposito spoke, "You've been very adamant about protecting Mrs. Montgomery, at quite a cost for you."

"Is there a question? I told you she took care of me."

"So, you owe her?"

Ellie understood at once where Valerie was going with this. For sure, Jamie's erratic behavior might be of a nature that had nothing to do with the horrific event in the past—or maybe it did.

"What do you need to protect her from, if she did nothing wrong?" she asked.

"People like you who won't leave her alone!"

"Jamie," Valerie said softly, "We all understand you're angry. Did Enid tell you she was worried or scared? Did she talk at all to you about George or Stella?"

"Stella was a freaking lesbian who came on to her," he spat.

Ellie's hand went to her neck, a reflexive gesture.

"I'm sorry, but I find that hard to believe," she said. "I saw the letters Stella wrote to George, and her diary. What really stood out what that Enid was behaving strangely—not because she was in love with her, but because she hated them both for it."

"It's disgusting. You're disgusting."

Enid Montgomery wasn't the only one who had gone through a troubling transformation since Ellie had first met her. She remembered sitting at the diner with Jamie, having a polite conversation. Both of them were acting paranoid, randomly aggressive.

"Enid told you, didn't she?"

"You don't have to answer that," Kellen reminded his client.

"That's why you panicked when the investigation was opened again. You'd rather go to prison than have her being held accountable."

"No, those are all lies!"

Esposito shrugged. "I see your client is not interested in co-operating. I guess this is it."

"Please, let me talk to Mr. Ryan in private for a moment."

"That won't change anything," Ryan said. "You want me to rat her out. I won't do it."

"Well…" Valerie got to her feet. "This is it, then. Have a good day."

Ellie followed her outside of the room, where Enid was still waiting a few feet further away.

"She did it," she said, aware that Enid was looking at her, smiling. "She killed Stella and then framed George for it. Two birds with one stone,"

"That's one way to put it," Valerie agreed. "But we can't prove it."

"There must be a way."

⁕

She had started out investigating a brutal murder. The story was a whole lot more complex than Ellie had imagined. She kept coming back to the intense relationship between Jamie and Enid. At this point, she was certain that he knew something. His various efforts to make them back off—they'd seemed clumsy and spontaneous, but what if they weren't?

It seemed like Jamie, who had at some point depended on Enid, still felt the same way—or he wanted her to know that she could depend on his loyalty in the present. It was clear that he loved her, that the loss of his parents, and her stepping in, had been a crucial moment in his life.

Perhaps she could find something looking into that accident once more, anything to make him reconsider. She touched her neck again where the bruises were still sensitive.

She wasn't looking to do him any favors after what he'd done. She wanted both of them to be held accountable for their respective crimes.

⁂

Ellie checked in with Lieutenant Carroll to inquire about Waters senior. The results of a toxicology screen had not yet come in, but he assured her that Cliff Waters' father was recovering.

Next, she did some more research on the accident that killed Ryan's parents, remembering what she'd learned before—no witnesses, no other vehicles on the street. The medical examiner had ruled an accident even under the circumstances, and now she wondered if they had made a mistake. Ryan was too young to remember anything about Stella Brown's murder, but his parents weren't.

She pushed her chair back, almost flinching at the conclusion. Did she really think that was what had happened? Did no one put the pieces together that way? She thought of the yearbook photos she'd seen of George, Stella, and Enid. Was it easier to believe that a man had committed a murder like this? She gave herself the answer. They operated on experience, knowledge and statistics. Most of the criminals she had arrested for this kind of crime were men. Was there a blind spot that had kept investigators from finding the truth in this case, for over decades?

"Hi, I'm glad to find you here. Is Jordan around?"

"Oh. Not at the moment. Hi, Kathryn."

There was a time when Jordan had not been happy to communicate with Kathryn, or have Ellie talk to her. In the present, they were in a place as good as they could possibly be, so she assumed it was okay.

"Can I help you with anything?"

"I wanted to check in and see if you two had time for lunch. And..." She lowered her voice, "How far along your plans are."

"Not that far yet," Ellie said. "I'm not sure when Jordan will be back, but you know what, I'm kind of hungry. I'll join you if it's okay."

Kathryn was surprised, but she seemed pleased.

"Of course it's okay. If you don't mind me asking, what happened to you? That looks painful."

"Suspect jumped at me yesterday. I'd like to say it's not as bad as it looks, but it really is."

"Yeah. A guy I dated choked me once like that. I'll always remember how that hurt."

Ellie winced at Kathryn's matter-of-fact delivery. She hated to think that any woman felt like that kind of behavior was something to be expected, hated even more that this was the kind of environment Jordan had grown up in. But this was a different time, for all of them.

"Well, the guy who did this will face consequences."

"That's good," Kathryn said. "Now where would you like to eat?"

❦

Jordan didn't have the time or appetite for lunch as she and Derek stood over the broken body of a man who had fallen from scaffolding on a construction site, the back of his head split open on the unyielding concrete.

"Foreman says he was a hard worker, no problems, no alcohol or drugs," Derek said.

"So, this was an accident? Any witnesses?"

"They were on a break. He said he'd join them later—when they came back, they found him like that."

"Really."

"That sounds like you don't believe it."

Jordan wasn't sure what she believed at this point, except that the sights and smells had an effect she wasn't used to. She looked up the scaffolding.

"Let's see if anything's up there," she suggested, and for the ME, she added, "When the techs are done down here, you can move him."

"Yeah, thanks," Dr. Adams said. "It's going to be one hell of a mess. Poor guy, I don't think he was coming to work thinking he'd be spilling his brains on the sidewalk..."

Given that she was only stating what they could all see clearly, Jordan was aware that her reaction was irrational. She couldn't help it and barely made it past the yellow tape and to the other side of some crates stacked high enough to give her some privacy.

After a few minutes, Derek appeared with a bottle of water, tissues and a pack of gum.

"Wow. Did I mention how much I appreciate you?"

"Not nearly often enough," he claimed. "I've never seen this happen before, so I have to ask. Is this a case for congratulations, or rather, stay far away from me?"

Jordan had to admit she'd pushed the thought as far from her mind as she possibly could, because she wasn't ready for the disappointment...It seemed unreal, especially since in the past twenty-four hours, she had been worried about Ellie's well-being more than anything else.

"Relax, I don't think it's either one. Stress, if anything. You saw those bruises Ryan gave Ellie."

Derek looked doubtful, but he didn't argue. "You want me to check the upper floor?"

Jordan took another sip of the water, then a deep breath.

"No thanks, I'll be okay."

"Sure?"

"Yes, I'm sure. Let's go."

What if?

She couldn't let herself be distracted by those thoughts or the lingering queasiness. One way or another, a big change was in the future, and until it was any less vague, she had to do her job. True, she didn't get sick at crime scenes, but it could have to do with all the changes she had made to prepare her body. She hoped it wasn't the virus Derek was worried about.

Regardless, she was grateful when they were back on the ground.

Nothing obvious as to what had led to the man's fall. Sometimes, things, good or bad, happened for no obvious reason.

She was still wondering.

⁂

Today could be the day. Any day could be the day they'd find out. Work had kept them apart for most of the time, so by the time Ellie turned off her computer, they hadn't exchanged more than a few text messages. Ellie's latest was to ask Jordan if she wanted to meet at the *SEVEN* for a quiet start into the weekend.

Sounds good, but let's meet at home first, okay? was Jordan's answer. She didn't elaborate. Maybe she didn't want to. Minutes later, Ellie sat in her car, stuck in traffic, tapping her fingers on the steering wheel. If there was something Jordan didn't want to discuss in public, it could mean only one thing. Ellie wanted to be home, though she wished she could come up with better words to say than the ones dancing on her mind.

I'm sorry. We'll try again. How many times would that work—and what would come after that? She wanted this baby with Jordan, so much, and she believed that they were more than ready to start a family. She would do whatever it took to make that happen. To her surprise, Ellie realized she felt anxious, regarding what implications this would have on their future, her future. Their plan, as it was, made perfect sense. She had proven herself in the unit, but her career was still just taking off. Jordan's perspective was a different one. She'd be so disappointed.

For a moment, Ellie considered stopping on the way to buy a bottle of wine, but she'd been sitting in traffic for too long already. And it wasn't really alcohol and distraction that Jordan needed. They had to talk seriously about a backup plan. Ellie had to get her head straight about what she was going to do, and why. Maybe there was a way. Casey had had her kids while working for the department, years ago.

She sighed in relief when the cars in front of her finally moved, and she could take her exit. She wasn't going to panic. It would be a long time before they ran out of options—and perhaps they would go to the *SEVEN*, enjoy the company of friends, have some good food and maybe even a beer. Her stomach rumbled as if in answer to her thoughts, making her chuckle.

We got this.

Almost home.

After unlocking the front door, Ellie went inside to find the lights were on in the living room and kitchen. Jordan's car sat in the parking spot, but it felt eerily quiet. Ellie hesitated, then spun around at the sound of a door closing.

"Hey. You're home," Jordan said as she came down the stairs. Ellie took in her appearance, trying to gauge the mood. Wearing black jeans and a white shirt, her hair in a ponytail, Jordan looked ready for an evening at *SEVEN*. Her expression was serious. Ellie didn't wait for any more information, just met her halfway and pulled her into a close embrace.

"I'm so sorry. I promise you, we'll find a way." She'd meant to be calm and reasonable, but apparently, that was out of the window now, her vision blurring.

"It's all right. It's going to happen," Jordan whispered.

It took a moment for the meaning of those words to sink in, and even when it did, Ellie didn't want to get ahead of herself. But Jordan wasn't the one crying. In fact, she sounded as calm and serene as Ellie had hoped to approach the subject.

"Are you saying what I think you're saying?" Ellie asked, reluctant to break the hug yet. Jordan gently disengaged herself, and they both sat on the steps.

"I don't even know why today. I had a little time, and I took the test and..." She laughed. "You'll think this is crazy. I couldn't believe it, so I went and got another one, and it said the same thing. I didn't want to tell you in a text message, and I didn't want anyone else around, in case...this." Her eyes were welling up. "It's for real."

As she took her hands, Ellie couldn't help thinking how she'd worried about coming home. Instead, this day turned out to be an affirmation. She couldn't think of words to express how grateful she was, but somehow, words weren't necessary.

They got up, and she followed Jordan back to the first floor to shower and change. Not much later, Ellie stood in front of the closet wearing bra and panties, Jordan being absolutely no help.

"I am amazed, and happy, but you're kind of distracting me."

"You're telling me?" Jordan asked, amused. "Do you have any idea how distracting you are?"

"It's the hormones," Ellie suggested. A split-second later she was secretly impressed with how quick Jordan was to move behind her, embracing her from behind.

"No. It's that I could never resist you," she corrected, fingertips teasing over naked skin. Ellie shivered with pleasure.

For sure, work and worrying about family planning hadn't left much time for intimacy lately. They didn't have time for this...did they?

"This one." Jordan picked a red dress and hung it over the door of the closet. "See, I helped you. That'll buy us a little time, right?"

She turned Ellie to her and leaned in to kiss her. Ellie's hunger was completely forgotten. The one for food, anyway.

Chapter Eighteen

Jordan had insisted on driving. Ellie didn't mind because it meant she could lean back and reminisce. Jordan's smile told her she was well aware what was on Ellie's mind.

"Fond memories?" she asked, keeping her eyes on the road.

"Now you're just smug."

"I thought I had a good reason. You said a few minutes ago your legs were still shaky."

Ellie took a deep breath. "Well, they were. I think I'll be good to drive home. Wow. I think we prepared well for this, but there are a lot of things we need to think about. Did you call the doctor?"

"Not yet. I'll do it tomorrow."

"Okay. We'll head over to Jack and Pauline's? Should we wait to tell anyone else?"

Jordan considered her question for a moment. "I don't think they'd be offended if someone else learns it first, but Derek has been chatting with Jack a lot lately."

"I'll keep that in mind. They're going to be so happy."

"Yeah." At a red light, Jordan cast her a quick, concerned look, well aware what was on Ellie's mind.

"I'm fine. Really. It sucks that they can't be here, but there are a lot of people who will be out of their minds with joy. It's good. Really."

"Okay. Now let's find out if anybody missed us."

As it turned out, their friends and family didn't seem to have expected them, if the surprised looks were any indication. Maria and Valerie sat at a table by themselves, and they found Derek and Kate with Casey, Sam, Libby and Wes. Ellie saw Jack and Pauline sharing a snack and wine in another, more private corner of the bar.

Jordan's gaze followed hers. "Yeah, it might be convenient tonight, but I'm not sure I want to spend all my Friday evenings in the same place as my parents."

"You're worried they catch you doing something naughty?" Derek, who had overheard her, asked. He chuckled realizing Ellie was flustered at his words. "Harding, you're too easy. I was joking. It's a pretty damn good place, and they own it. Told you they should have called it Carpenter's. Oh, and here." He set a couple of beer bottles in front of them. "We haven't seen you here in ages."

"You're exaggerating," Jordan said. "I'm fine, but Ellie can have those. I think she might need them."

"But I promised I'd keep you company during your alcohol abstinence."

"That's okay. Go ahead. I might hold you to it later."

Derek was only half-following their exchange, the hints a bit too subtle, but Casey leaned over to say, "Hey. Congrats. This is great news."

"I'm hearing great news," Kate chimed in. "What is it?"

She squealed a bit when Ellie revealed it to her. Casting a look over at Jack and Pauline's table, Ellie realized they were still immersed in their conversation.

182

Jordan felt like on a high, and she was determined to allow the emotion for the time being. Soon after their wedding, Natalie Morgan had come along, presenting a multitude of challenges to them...and they had barely arrested her when going straight for the next big thing. Truth be told, she had tried to ignore the subject at times, then be terrified that the outcome might always be the same. Yes, there was still a long way ahead, but they weren't talking about maybe, someday, anymore.

Hormones might have had a little to do with it, but she'd felt the sudden and overwhelming need to be close to Ellie when she'd watched her rummaging through her closet half-naked. Every so often, she was still amazed how life had worked out for them so far, finding love, a home, becoming a family. All of this was so much more than she'd ever envisioned for herself, and what she felt for Ellie was so much more than she'd ever considered herself capable of. The close calls they'd had between them only made the present moment more miraculous and beautiful.

"Excuse me for a second," she said to her cheering friends, giving Ellie's hand a tug. "I think we're doing this right now."

They both sat down at Jack and Pauline's table. Jordan thought that she might not have to say anything, because she was radiating happiness to an extent they might guess...but the news wasn't that obvious to everyone.

"The place is busy," she said. "You've really done a great job. You plan on being around?"

Jack laughed. "Is this the moment that you tell us it's slightly awkward to hang out in the same place as your parents?"

"No. This is the moment..." All of a sudden, she wasn't sure she could get out the words. Ellie laid her hand over hers. "The moment where I was wondering if you could make time to babysit sometime in the future."

They both seemed speechless, seconds ticking by.

"Is it true?" Pauline caught her off guard as she started to cry.

"Mom, please, don't do that." Most of her closest friends knew and loved her parents, but at some point, Jordan would be worried about her reputation—her own eyes were welling up, a sensation that had become all too familiar since the second test. "Don't cry?"

Both Jack and Pauline got to her feet, and hugged her, and then Ellie.

They had never answered her question, but she assumed since Pauline had raised the subject on the day she first brought Ellie to dinner, it shouldn't be a problem.

❦

"We have to think of a name. We can probably make it without daycare, but we should start a college fund in case."

Jordan couldn't help laughing. "You're aware that there's lots of time for all of those things, right?"

There had been no more nausea, on the contrary. She felt happy and at home in her body, and even though they couldn't celebrate with champagne, they had definitely honored the happy occasion in other ways. Ellie, now in a nightgown, was sitting up against the headboard, watching her dress for the night.

"I'm aware," she said. "But that time goes by fast. Faster since the day I met you, it seems."

"I know what you mean. Still, I think we can wait a little with the college fund. I made an appointment. I guess I'll have to talk to the lieutenant soon."

"Are you worried about that?" Ellie asked, ever observant. "There are rules in place. He's not the type to cause any problems over this."

"No, I'm not worried about that." She thought of Shriver, wanting that job so badly. "Like Casey said, the department can accommodate. It just means a lot of changes, but that's okay. This is what we want."

"Yes, it is."

For all her life, Jordan had been afraid to jinx anything good, by bad luck or something of her own doing—but when Ellie was fast asleep, she stayed awake, allowing herself to dream of the future.

Chapter
Nineteen

Reality caught up with her quickly when she sat across from the construction worker's grieving husband. A happy couple, they had planned to buy a house—one of them being a builder, the other an electrician, they'd been excited to do a lot of work themselves.

There was no nefarious reason for his death—he had stayed behind, working overtime with the upcoming purchase in mind, and slipped. His colleagues were shell-shocked. No one had given him any grief for being married to a man.

"We don't often deal with random shit like that. God, doesn't that make you want to quit and do everything you ever wanted to do in life?" Derek shook himself.

"What is it that you want to do?" Jordan asked, curious. She, too, felt like there might be a somber life lesson here, though her life had already become so much more, with Ellie, than she ever imagined.

"I don't know, buy a boat?"

"A boat?" she echoed. In all the years they'd worked together, she'd never heard him talk like this.

"Yeah, why not? Up in Canada, Kate and I went sailing with some friends of hers. We were talking about it. Or an RV maybe. I always wanted to travel cross-country."

"I had no idea. You should do it, then."

"What about you?"

"Me? I'm going to have a baby. That's as big a deal as it gets for me."

"I get that, but at some point, that baby is going to head off to college. Anything else you or Ellie want to scratch off the list?"

"I think she'd really like to prove that the homophobic senior citizen committed a murder, and her grandnephew is lying for her...aside from that...we're good now. But you should really look into that boat."

"Yeah. Later tonight, for sure."

❦

By the time Ariel's sleepover came around, Jamie Ryan had been denied bail, Kate and Derek were looking at actual boats, and Jordan and Ellie had confirmation from Jordan's doctor.

All of a sudden, the no caffeine, no alcohol rule was a lot easier to follow, though with Becca Crane's warning, they were careful to keep their enthusiasm in check.

Ariel seemed in a good mood though when she arrived, her hair still damp from the shower she had taken after her track practice.

"Thanks so much for taking me in for the weekend," she said, beaming. "I think Becca didn't feel okay leaving me alone."

Jordan held back her surprise. Either Ariel didn't want to address her reluctance to stay anywhere else overnight, or Becca had bent the truth a little. Either way, she could understand why both of them clung a bit, after everything Ariel had been through.

"You're welcome, in any case," she said when they were on their way to dinner. Ariel's choice. "So, what have you been up to?"

"Running, mostly. They put me on the team." Ariel shrugged. "Apparently I'm really fast."

"Wow, that's great, congratulations!" Jordan could sympathize. At Ariel's age, she, too, had found refuge in athletic achievements.

"I guess it's cool." When they had rescued Ariel from the cult, she'd been a frightened child, strong, but trying to escape from a world of trauma, her mother's death, the things she had seen. It was refreshing to see her act like a typical teenager.

"What about you?" she asked.

"Different things," Jordan said vaguely, not wanting to break the big news before they had gotten some food. "Right now, I'm starving. Let's see if our table is ready?"

It wasn't until much later that she figured that this conversation might be a more difficult one than she had imagined. They were seated fairly close to a family of four, one of which was a crying baby. While Jordan had a fleeting thought that she and Ellie might be those parents not long from now, Ariel gave the scene a quick, dark look. Jordan was reminded of her testimony against the cult members. She had dared what many grown women living with the Prophets of Better Days had been too afraid to do.

Taking care of the younger children was mandatory, until the girls got married themselves—and beyond.

"This is so annoying," Ariel commented. "Can we have another table? What if it's like that all night?"

"I think we'll be fine."

"Please? That's all I listened to, all the time. I'm so glad you got me out before they made me have one."

"I can ask," Ellie offered. They silently agreed that this was a subject for another day.

Jordan hoped Ariel wouldn't feel let down, but she had to understand that they would always be there for her—and the context in which their baby was born, would be completely different from the one she'd grown up in.

When Ariel went back home, they hadn't addressed the baby question with her, and perhaps there would be a better time to do that, Ellie reflected.

The day Jamie Ryan pled guilty, Enid Montgomery called her. After giddily browsing websites of baby clothes, the call startled her. She wished she could have done more, but there were no more avenues for her to try. Waters senior was feeling as well as possible under the circumstances—the tox screen had shown no interference with his medication or any other red flags. It wasn't like Jamie Ryan was innocent. Her fading bruises reminded her of that.

"I was hoping you could come by."

"I'm not sure what that would accomplish, Enid. I'm sorry." Of course she was curious. Ellie didn't think it would do anything good to see the woman.

"Maybe I overreacted. About Stella. I miss her every day, you know, even with all the faults she possessed. And George...I had no idea how much I'd miss him too."

Ellie refrained from saying, *that's too bad*, although for a brief moment, she'd been tempted.

"I'm sorry it had to come to this," she repeated. "But you know what Jamie did. He fired at me and attacked me at the station."

"Yes, I'm aware of that." Enid sounded rueful. "You know, he wasn't always that way. He was such a happy child…He changed after his parents died. And all this time…He's felt this obligation to protect me. If anyone criticizes me, he feels it's an attack." That much was obvious to Ellie, though she wasn't sure what to say. She wasn't a therapist. It was obvious that both Enid and Jamie Ryan could use one.

"Enid, what are you hoping this will achieve?"

"Maybe it will give both of us peace. I'm frankly tired."

Ellie was hearing several things in the unexpected confession. Enid's long-held façade seemed to be cracking. Did that mean she was ready to make revelations? Did it mean she was dangerous?

The gun was registered in Jamie's name, but that didn't mean she didn't have a weapon. Ellie didn't want to be paranoid or underestimate the woman she still suspected to have murdered her friend. Arriving with blazing sirens probably wouldn't make her comfortable enough to talk. Ellie wasn't about to take chances either, especially now that she and Jordan were going to be parents.

"Okay, I'll be over in about an hour."

She asked Sam, and Wes, who was riding with her for the time being, to join her.

Chapter Twenty

"You don't trust me," Enid stated when she looked at the squad car parked on the other side of the street. "Is it because I don't agree with some people's lifestyles? Yours, I imagine?"

Ellie shook her head. "That's not what I'm here for. You said you had something important to tell me."

"Why don't we sit down, have some tea? You seemed to enjoy my cookies on other occasions."

Ellie sat, tense. At this point she wasn't sure whether it was safe to accept food or beverages from the woman.

"What was it you wanted to tell me? I thought everything was quite clear."

"You think I killed Stella."

"Does it matter what I think? The case is obviously closed now."

"Yes, because you couldn't come up with any new evidence...Something you would have liked so much, because I offended you. Maybe I offended Stella as well. That's not the same as murder, is it, Detective?"

"People do horrible things prompted by their misguided beliefs," Ellie said. "This isn't achieving anything. I'm beginning to think you just called me here so you can sic your lawyer on me again. I'm sorry, Enid. I'm sorry for everything that went so wrong in your life it made you think you have to blame people who have nothing to do with it. Who have done nothing wrong."

"That's quite a speech, dear. Let me get you that tea. Everything is easier with a nice, warm beverage."

Ellie noticed that Enid wasn't struggling at all to get up, and she wasn't using her cane as she went into the kitchen. She didn't have any problems carrying the small tray either.

"Have some," she said. "I'm afraid you're going to need something comforting." She laughed when she saw Ellie's hand go to her gun.

"Come on, how stupid do you think I am? With your colleagues right across the street? Wasn't I smart enough to frame George for Stella's murder? You think I'm not so sharp anymore?"

"I think Jamie has been in denial for a long time, or he wouldn't defend you so forcefully."

"Poor Jamie."

"I don't know about that. He is an adult. He's responsible for his own actions now. Can I ask you why? I assume that since you asked me here, you want to tell your side of the story."

"Oh, you did a great job figuring it all out by yourself, didn't you? Just too bad you can't prove any of it. Look, I did what I had to do. George was...convenient in any way."

"You were attracted to Stella."

"Aren't you clever, dear? I knew that if I ever wanted to have a chance at a normal life, I needed her out of the way."

"But that didn't work, did it?" Ellie asked, feeling sick. "Because there were other women you were attracted to, and you just kept on hating them, and hating yourself."

"Silly, I didn't have time to chase after women. I had Jamie to take care of. It's too bad, the things he got himself into, time after time. I really tried to be a good role model for him, for everything he gave me."

"The 'normal' life." Ellie suppressed a shudder. "You murdered Stella, because you were attracted to her, and you murdered Jamie's parents so you could play house? And everyone would think you're so amazing, for taking care of your family, and forgiving George. You got all the credit."

"I deserved to be free."

There was a gleam in Enid's eyes, and Ellie knew that nothing she could say would ever reach the woman. She had to give it one more shot anyway.

"I understand that things would have been much more complicated sixty years ago, but you could have found someone. Stella was straight—but even if she was stringing you along, she didn't deserve to die. You could have been in a relationship and have a child. You didn't need to kill to be free."

"Look who's talking. Your generation had everything handed to you, even the idea that unnatural is now normal. I bet you even got married. It's despicable." She almost spat those words.

"You know I'm going to arrest you, Enid. You murdered three people, and made an innocent man serve a lifetime sentence. Who's the despicable one now?"

Enid smiled. "You can't arrest me. What would that look like, put a senior citizen into prison? You have no proof, nothing. I'll deny everything I said."

"Yeah, well, good luck with that," Ellie said as she took out her cell phone and showed it to Enid who blanched.

"I've had my colleagues and an A.D.A. on conference call. Honestly, I wasn't sure this would work out, but you couldn't wait to gloat to me, could you?"

"You tricked me. This will never hold up in court. I don't even know what I'm saying sometimes—you can't use any of it."

"Let me worry about that. Let's go."

⁂

After her shift, Ellie met Jill Allen at Doreen Byrd's house to share the news. Doreen hugged her close, in tears.

"I don't know how to thank you both," said. "It took so long."

Ellie shared a look with Jill who looked pensive. Too long for George Wilder, but at least his name would be cleared. There would be some accountability, and possibly, Enid Montgomery would spend the rest of her days in prison.

Ellie wanted to go home, spend the weekend dreaming about the future—but there was something else she needed to do first. She left a message, knowing well that she'd risk another confirmation, but she thought there was someone else who deserved to be updated.

Cliff Waters met her in the lobby, wearing a stony expression. She hoped that for once, he'd control his temper. It was dinner time. She didn't plan on staying long.

Joe Waters looked aged, but he was obviously back to participating in daily activities and having his meals with the other residents.

"Detective Harding, it's so nice to see you again. I'll admit I've missed you. This was the most excitement I've had in years."

"Mr. Waters." She shook his hand. "I won't be long. I just wanted you to know that we arrested Enid Montgomery. You've helped me a great deal."

"It was my pleasure. Come by any time you'd like to bounce off ideas. See, Cliff, your old man could actually be helpful with something. Your colleague here has a bright future ahead."

"Yeah, and she doesn't mind destroying the future of a good cop—again."

Ellie assumed he was talking about Atwood. She hadn't heard any news—and she wasn't going to take the bait either.

"I'll leave you two to it now. Have a nice evening, Mr. Waters."

"No, wait a minute, Cliff, you can't just make accusations like that."

"I can when it's the truth," he seethed.

"This is really not the place, but if you mean Chris Atwood, he was the backup that never arrived. That's not a good cop, I'm sorry."

"Fuck you and the high horse you—"

"Cliff!" his father interrupted him sharply. "Don't you think you've done enough? I want you to leave."

"Dad!"

"You heard me. Come back when you're ready to take responsibility for your actions."

Red-faced, Waters turned away and stalked out of the room. Ellie stood, unsure what to say.

"He's my son, and I love him, but right now, I'm not proud of him."

That didn't make it easier.

"I understand it's difficult but thank you again for your help."

"You're leaving already? I was hoping you could tell me a bit more."

Ellie decided there was no reason she couldn't spend a bit more time with him.

"Do you think there's a chance I could snatch something from that buffet again?" she asked, and he chuckled.

"Absolutely."

Ellie walked away with many things still on her mind. Some loose ends, she just had to let them be. Much as she sympathized with the older Waters, she couldn't solve the conflict he had with his son. She'd caught a lucky break when she'd realized that Enid was eager to brag about what she'd done and give her chilling confession.

George and Stella were together now, and the real murderer would face consequences. Justice, poetic and otherwise, had come late for them, but it was finally served.

When she arrived home, Ellie was surprised to find Jordan sitting at the table with Ariel, sharing a pizza.

"We left you some, in case you were hungry," Jordan said.

There was an air of relief about her that made Ellie curious before Ariel got up and hugged her close.

"I already said congratulations to Jordan," she said. "On the baby," she added as if that was necessary. Over her shoulder, Ellie gave Jordan a surprised look.

"I wasn't sure how long you'd be working, so I asked Ariel over for dinner. And...we've been looking at baby names."

"You'll be great parents," Ariel said. "You're caring people. I know you are."

"Thank you. I had dinner with Mr. Waters, but I'm really curious what names you came up with?"

Ellie sat with them, grateful for the present moment and the promise the future held for all of them.

About the Author

B arbara Winkes writes sapphic crime drama and Christmas romance. She loves writing characters who get the job done, whether it's stopping a predator or saving cherished traditions—while still making time for love. She lives with her wife in Quebec City.

barbarawinkes.com

Also by Barbara Winkes

Luce Allen Mysteries
In Harm's Way
Under Pressure

The Crossing Lines Trilogy
Undercover
Redemption
Vengeance

The Connected Series
Promised to the Queen
Drawn to the Enemy
Tempted by the Protector
Saved by the Heiress

Carpenter/Harding
Indiscretions
Insinuations
Incisions
Intrusions

Initiations
Intentions
Infatuations
Impressions
Implications
Infractions
Incidents
Illusions

Kelli & Merin Romantic Suspense
Thunder
Rain

Lord and Burton
Clean Slate

Standalone
The Amnesia Project